STATIONARY ORBIT

STATIONARY ORBIT

by

Peter Macey

London
DENNIS DOBSON

First published in Great Britain in 1974
by Dobson Books Ltd, 80 Kensington Church Street, London W8
Printed by Willmer Brothers Limited, Birkenhead

ISBN 0 234 77121 6

To B.

Chapter one

Although the main events are now part of history the full story of the incidents leading up to that incredible confrontation has never been told. But it all started in such a very small way, and apart from Prof I was the only person in it right from the beginning.

'The Department of Interstellar Communication' does sound an impressive title but at that time it consisted of two small sheds on the edge of the University playing fields, one containing a modest collection of electronic bits and pieces still in the manufacturers' cardboard boxes, the other ready to serve as an office.

I had applied for a place in the cybernetics research project as soon as I got my degree, but Professor Gannet said there were too many people with firsts for them to look at a lower second. It was only what I'd expected I suppose and I wasn't really cut out for research, but life at college was very pleasant, Beryl wasn't finishing until next year, and the three interviews I'd been to hadn't resulted in any other job so far. Anyway I had packed my trunk and bought my ticket home and was just drinking my last cup of refectory coffee when in comes Professor Gannet, in person.

'Have you got a job yet, Brendon?' he barks. 'Have you got anything fixed up?'

'No sir.' I had to admit to my unemployed status.

'Well no one's applied for the grant to work in the DIC. Can't understand why. But it's yours if you want it.'

I knew what DIC stood for and I knew why nobody had applied for the grant. It was a standing joke around the place; you don't get many profs with a bee that size in their bonnets. However, I couldn't afford to be choosy could I?

'Interstellar Communication, sir?'

'Yes Brendon. What do you think of that for an opportunity?'

Actually I didn't think much. 'How would I communicate?' I protested. 'I've only got three years to get my Ph.D. If I send off some kind of message now it'll take ages for them to get it, even assuming there is someone out there, and by the time the answer's come back . . .' I had a momentary vision of a white-haired old research student busily decoding in a corner of the shed.

'No Brendon,' said the Prof pityingly, 'you don't ring them. They ring you.'

I stared at him in stunned silence. 'Do they?'

'It's my belief there are messages coming in all the time from other solar systems; the radio telescope picks up an enormous amount of radiation from all over the sky. The only problem is interpretation, and that's where you come in isn't it?'

'I shan't be able to speak their language sir.' I wondered whether Professor Gannet could be an undiscovered schizophrenic but I decided it might be difficult to tell with a prof, so I gave him the benefit of the doubt.

'Of course you can speak their language Brendon. If they're intelligent enough to try to communicate they'll know they've got to use the universal language.'

So he was off his rocker. 'A sort of galactic Esperanto?' I suggested doubtfully.

'Of course not,' thundered Professor Gannet. 'It sounds as if you've been reading too much science fiction.'

I apologized.

'The universal language is mathematics, Brendon, mathematics, logic, algebra, numerology. You will be looking for a message in numbers, not in letters. And don't go assuming they've got ten fingers like us.'

'No sir.' I did understand this last bit. 'I will send all my messages in binary notation.'

'Well thank goodness I've got through to you at last. I was beginning to wonder if you were capable of communicating with anyone.'

I looked suitably penitent.

'I've arranged for you to have tapes of the signals from the telescope to start with,' he went on, 'while you're building your own amplifier, but the sooner you're independent of them the

2

better. They're very sceptical about this project.' Personally I didn't blame them.

'You can't put radio-frequencies on tape,' I protested.

'No,' explained Prof scathingly, 'the tapes will just have the low-frequency component won't they, not the carrier wave?'

Not very hopefully I enquired about technical assistance, but Professor Gannet didn't think much of that idea.

'You know how to use a soldering-iron don't you Brendon?'

It was going to be an interesting dialogue—Harold Brendon and the rest of the universe.

Beryl thought I must be mad. 'You'll never get a Ph.D out of it you know. I think you should go into industry,' she said.

She was right about me not getting a Ph.D, but I still think I might have had a chance if the War Office hadn't made me cut out all those bits they said infringed the Official Secrets Act.

Although it was a distinctly way-out topic I was keen to begin research as soon as possible and Prof said there was no need to wait until term started in October, but at the last moment I got a vacation job with 'Information Storage Ltd.' It wasn't as exciting as it sounds because my principal duties seemed to be making tea and posting letters but I earned a few pounds and at the end of August I left to come back and start communicating.

Despite what Gannet had said I found the radio telescope people very co-operative; at least they were once they'd got all the jokes about little green men off their chests. They provided me with miles of tape which I had to look at on the oscilloscope, and try and analyse on the computer.

Gannet had arranged for me to have access to the computer for ten minutes a day, from 1–15 to 1–25 a.m. That would clobber my love-life once and for all I thought, not that my love-life had been anything worth clobbering so far, but there was always hope.

When I started going with Beryl people used to give me knowing winks, nudge me in the ribs, and say, 'You'll be all right there you know.' It made me furious. She was such a sweet girl and I thought she was the most affectionate person

3

I'd ever met. I know she was very fond of me but we never seemed to make much progress. I think it was because I couldn't ever get her on her own; my digs were usually full of people, and the two girls who shared Beryl's flat always seemed to be having an early night when I was there.

I didn't have to work nights though. I just used to leave the programmes and tapes at the computer centre when I left in the evening and the wave analyses were ready for me in the morning. That was just as well because the computer spewed out so much paper in ten minutes that it took me until about 4 o'clock in the afternoon just to read through it.

My office measured fifteen feet by twelve and contained one desk, one chair, one empty filing cabinet, and a bookcase with my five books. Prof said there'd be room for six research students when the time came to expand the project, and I think he pictured a sort of nerve centre of the universe, with messages from outer space pouring in night and day, but I couldn't see it myself.

Anyway I spent every morning and half of every afternoon either peering at the oscilloscope screen or ploughing through a sort of gigantic toilet roll about fifteen inches wide, bored to desperation. Several times a day my mind would seize up in a panic. The days and weeks were going by and there wasn't a glimmer of a sign of anything to fill even half a page of a Ph.D thesis.

A more interesting part of the day's work was the hour or two I had to spare for working on the amplifier and I was quite good with a soldering-iron, though not as good as Derek Sandgate, the Prof's personal research assistant. When he wasn't attending a conference in San Francisco or a symposium in Rome Professor Gannet directed the researches of about sixteen Ph.D students. In addition he had a little pet line of his own, and for that he needed the services of a very good technician, one who really was good with a soldering-iron. Sam West in the stores once told me that when the Prof wanted to join two wires together he used a reef knot, which was presumably why Derek had to make sure that Prof never laid a finger on any of the actual apparatus.

'Are you going up to three hundred?' Derek had enquired,

4

strolling into my one-man department one afternoon soon after the beginning of term.

'Three hundred?' I wasn't quite with it yet.

'Megacycles. You should you know, and you could with that kit there.'

'I haven't designed the circuit yet but I'd like to cover as big a range as I can. It won't be very directional so I've got to keep away from the broadcasting bands. I don't want to be picking up the Third Programme.'

'You'd never decipher that. You want to be over two hundred megacycles, but I can give you a hand if you like because we haven't got much on up in the penthouse.' Professor Gannet's lab was on the top floor.

I was grateful for this help but more than a little worried in case Prof found out. He'd have gone berserk. It was rather like an ordinary seaman on HMS Victory accepting personal favours from Lady Hamilton.

'Gannet's in Tokyo till next Wednesday, and I've finished all the work he left me so I might as well give you a hand. I'm rather taken with this idea of interstellar communication you know.'

It was refreshing to find one other person besides the Professor who didn't think what I was doing was a complete waste of time. I learned that Derek was an avid reader of the more picturesque kind of science fiction, and he believed every word he read. He didn't just think there might possibly be some kind of intelligent life on other planets; he had a vivid picture of bug-eyed monsters wrestling with giant alien supermen, of eight-legged space pirates, colonies of intelligent ants, and civilizations a million years ahead of ours. But still enthusiasm is always better than apathy isn't it? And he really was a genius with that soldering-iron.

Derek's help more than doubled my rate of progress with the amplifier but it did nothing to relieve the tedium of sorting through the computer analysis of the telescope tapes. It would have driven me up the wall if it hadn't been for the relief of meeting Beryl for a cup of coffee every morning and afternoon, but even that posed certain problems.

'Couldn't you make sure you come down at a regular time, Harold?'

'Whatever for?' I asked. 'They serve coffee all the morning.'

'Well I have a cup with George Venner at half past ten, and after that I'm usually talking to Ken Stannage until nearly eleven. If you could manage to come down just after eleven we can be on our own for ten minutes then.'

I did wish Beryl hadn't been quite so popular. It wouldn't have mattered if she'd had more work to do, but while other people could just manage fifteen minutes in between lectures Beryl held court in the refectory for upwards of an hour each morning. You'd think taking an honours maths degree was a full-time job wouldn't you? But as well as being the sexiest eyeful in the Science Faculty Beryl was a mathematical genius, so that two or three hours a day was all the work she needed to do. It was very difficult, and over and over again I tried to throw my cards in. I thought of making my own coffee in the office but Beryl was desolate.

'Harold darling. Wherever were you yesterday? It was absolutely dead down here and I was ever so worried that something might have happened to you. You haven't fallen for someone else have you sweetheart?'

Beryl's hand slipped into mine under the table, her leg pressed against my thigh, and we sipped our coffee in utter bliss. She was so warm-hearted and I knew she liked me. If only I could get her to my digs one evening when the other three were out. My mind reeled at the intoxicating prospect. Should I suggest Saturday? Beryl looked up into my face.

'Harold darling, I have to rush. The engineers come down at quarter past eleven.'

Back in the Department of Interstellar Communication Derek was waiting, his eyes sparkling with eagerness to tell me what was obviously a great piece of news. I tried to shed my gloom because I hate to dampen enthusiasm.

'Have you heard the news? He's gone to Canberra—for three weeks.'

'Professor Gannet?' I enquired.

'Yes. To the international conference on communication

6

satellites—for three weeks, and he hasn't left me a thing to do.'

'You haven't told him you're helping me?'

'No of course not. He wouldn't stand for that. He thinks I'm helping out in the stores, but there's nothing to do down there. I thought I could make a start running that cable round the field for you.'

After a lot of careful thought I had decided to fit up an aerial with an untuned pre-amplifier on the far side of the playing-field, next to the park where there would be the minimum of interference, and then run a co-axial cable along the fence by the pool at the edge of the zoo and across to the lab. That was going to take a lot of cable. It would cost a fortune and I hadn't even got the estimate through yet, as I pointed out to my willing helper.

It didn't put Derek off though. 'That's my other piece of news. Co-ax cable. It's been in the back of the stores ever since the University Training Corps was disbanded. I've got it on indefinite loan.'

I was still spending all my mornings trying to make sense of the computer's interpretation of the bursts of radiation the radio telescope picked up, but three weeks of Derek working full-time and me part-time more or less saw the receiver finished, well the Mark One prototype at any rate. By the time the last wire was soldered in Professor Gannet was back and Derek was kept busy up in the penthouse, but I saved the inauguration ceremony until one afternoon when he could slip down while the Prof was giving his one weekly lecture. I let Derek switch on.

'I name this receiver "Earth Station One". May it represent the first step in the development of true interstellar harmony and understanding.'

'Splendid,' I laughed. 'Charles himself couldn't have done better. You're wasted as a technician.'

We gazed at the oscilloscope screen in awed dismay. I'd decided that a visual presentation would be best at this stage but the confusion of green flashes and waves was more like abstract art than an intelligible signal.

7

'You mean Picasso couldn't have done better, don't you?' suggested Derek. 'Seriously though, that's noise isn't it?'

I knew what he meant—random background, the bugbear of all electronic equipment. 'The gain's too high.'

We turned down the gain and had a horizontal straight line. We turned it up and observed abstract masterpieces of electronic pyrotechnics.

'Signal to noise ratio,' commented Derek.

'What signal?' I asked.

'Perhaps the computer could dig something out.'

But I'd had enough of that; I was determined to concentrate on an electronic solution. Of course we'd only looked at one wavelength so far but going through the other wavelengths proved to be very time-consuming, and after the novelty had worn off even more tedious than the computer's roll of toilet paper.

We fixed up a motor drive to scan the receiver's waveband from one end to the other with infinite slowness, while I sat staring at the screen until I felt sure my eyes would drop out. I can't tell you the actual wavelengths we were working on because that was one of the things the War Office were so sticky about when they gave me permission to publish this, although I don't see why they should have worried. It was just red-tape I suppose. Anyway it was very tiring and I was a physical wreck by the time I packed it in at five o'clock. That's why I made such a mess of my first real opportunity to get Beryl on her own.

'Harold darling, why don't you come round to my flat for a bit of supper tonight? Joan and Chloe are both going out.'

'I'd love to. What time shall I be there?' I had planned to spend the evening translating a paper on the ionosphere out of 'Naturwissenschaften', but this would obviously take priority over that.

'How about eight o'clock? The others will both be gone by then, and we can have a nice little chat while you sample my Spaghetti Bolognese.'

At two minutes to eight I was ringing Beryl's door-bell and by five minutes past I was sitting on the settee while Beryl plied me with evidence of her culinary expertise. I marvelled that so much beauty and talent could be packed into a mere eight and a half stone of flesh and blood.

'It's all out of tins you know,' she explained. 'I'm so glad you could come though. I was going to the Hallé with the others, but Jack Willis who was taking me sprained his ankle yesterday so he had to miss it. I was at an absolute loose end and I know you don't like Shostakovitch so I thought you'd rather come here.'

You wouldn't find many girls as completely honest as that would you? She was always thinking of other people as well, and trying to remember what they liked. I'd only mentioned once that I didn't like modern Russian composers.

'Have another vanilla slice, Harold. They'll only be wasted.' Her slender white hand brushed a lock of soft black hair from in front of a large wistful eye.

'No thanks. I really couldn't manage anything else. I'll help you take the things into the kitchen.'

Five minutes later we were sitting on the settee again. Beryl rested her head on my shoulder and I stroked her long black hair. The warm atmosphere had lulled my brain, exhausted by a long day at the oscilloscope, into a drowsy euphoria, but the exciting animal presence of Beryl stirred my body into passionate wakefulness.

'You're very beautiful, Beryl.'

'Harold.'

I gently kissed her cheek; a faint but intoxicating perfume filled my head. She twisted her face towards mine and I kissed her lips. I felt her soft body pressed against my chest and I gently undid the two small buttons on her shoulder. I shivered with excitement as we drew apart slightly and Beryl looked up into my face.

'Harold my darling, would you mind ever so much if we just watched a programme on the television? It's about the environment and I think that's so important nowadays, don't you?'

Beryl was a very serious-minded girl, and I don't think I'd ever have wanted anyone without a social conscience, but just then I did find it very difficult to concentrate on the television.

9

'The population explosion is the most important social force of this century,' agreed Beryl, echoing the words of the television announcer. 'I think everyone should use contraceptives. I've been on the pill ever since I've been up at college,' she added.

I was taken aback but I don't know why, because I had been bothering all day about how far we might get, and what precautions I ought to take, and Beryl's preparedness meant I didn't have to worry. I knew she wasn't going to draw back at the last moment either, but if she'd been on the pill for two years what did that make me? Just one more in a very long queue. But I didn't just want Beryl for an evening's pleasure; I loved her and I wanted her for ever. I thought of all those others, coarse promiscuous louts. Dirty? Diseased? I shuddered at the thought of how one of them might have infected her.

I think Beryl sensed my misgivings. She smiled kindly and touched my face.

'I love you Harold.'

She wasn't necessarily a tramp was she? Perhaps she'd been on the pill all this time just as a precaution, just in case she met someone. I might even be the first.

Beryl snuggled up against my cheek and we clung together watching the television screen. It was larger than the oscilloscope screen, and black and white instead of greenish. The pattern of light was less random, but the pain at the back of my head was just the same. I closed my eyes and pulled Beryl closer to me. A man was being interviewed in the television studio. His voice was low and monotonous. I heard it droning on but the words did not come through. I seemed to be sliding down a long soft gentle slope into oblivion.

'Hello Beryl. How did the cooking go?'

'A great success. How was the Hallé?'

'Fantastic. The Berlioz was out of this world.'

What was happening? Who were all these people? The realization struck me between the eyes—I'd fallen asleep—I'd been sitting on the settee with Beryl and I'd fallen asleep. I blinked hard and tried to summon instant wakefulness.

'Hello Joan. Hello Chloe. How was the Shostakovitch?'

10

'Rather square I'm afraid, a bit of his party-line period.'

If Beryl's room-mates had noticed that I was asleep they were very very tactful about it, and Beryl herself was absolutely wonderful.

'We've had a fabulous time up here, just the two of us. And Harold thinks my vanilla slices are three star cordon bleu.'

'I think I'd better be getting back,' I said miserably.

Beryl came to the front door with me.

'Oh Beryl, I'm so sorry,' I almost wept.

'Don't worry. I didn't mind. You were tired out weren't you?'

'You should have woken me up. You should have slapped my face and brought me round.'

'But you needed the sleep, my love, and I didn't mind. There was an old film on I hadn't seen and I got quite engrossed in it. It was lovely having you there beside me and you didn't snore you know.'

I was still paralysed with the humiliation.

'Aren't you going to kiss me goodnight?'

I took her in my arms and she melted into a warm bundle of soft lovingness. I felt the contour of her breast through her thin blouse and her tongue deliciously ran round my lips. I wondered how far one could go in the porchway of a block of flats.

'I shall have to be going back up now Harold darling.'

Beryl gently pulled herself away and ran lightly up the stairs.

'Goodnight sweetheart,' I called sadly.

But I knew it would be all right next time.

It was the week after that I finished scanning the waveband on the oscilloscope. It was something that had to be cleared up out of the way and I just threw myself into it, staying in the lab until about ten every night. Derek was with me in the middle of one afternoon when the scanning motor covered the last megacycle and automatically cut off.

'So much for that little idea then, Derek,' I said, rubbing my bloodshot red-ringed eyes.

'There might be a signal there below the noise level though, mightn't there?'

'There might very well be, and I'll tell you this much. If there is I'm going to dig it out. I know this is a hair-brained project but it's the sort of challenge that makes me determined to beat the odds. I've never been better than mediocre in anything I tried so far and the only way to make anyone notice me is to do something that's definitely impossible.'

Actually I had reached the point where I think even Professor Gannet would have allowed me to pack it in and go on to something else and it was probably frustration over Beryl as much as anything that made me so determined; I'd asked her out half a dozen times since that disastrous night I fell asleep and every time she'd got something else on, but she was so friendly I knew she wasn't just making up excuses.

'Are you going to sharpen up the tuning?' suggested Derek.

'That's more or less the idea.'

'We've got most of the standard circuit designs incorporated.'

'I know but I have got one or two other ideas although I don't think they'll be enough to do the trick on their own. Any signal from intelligence outside the solar system is bound to be pathetically weak by the time it reaches us.'

'We've had it then.'

'Not quite. I've just got one ace up my sleeve—a dual receiver.'

Derek nodded in understanding, 'They'll both be picking up the same signal, if there is one, but the random noise which they both have will be different.'

'That's right. We rig up another dipole out on the edge of the park with a separate cable back to the lab. The two cables can run alongside most of the way because they'll both be screened. Then we need a stage to take the output from both channels and eliminate everything that's not common to both. What's left we amplify and amplify and amplify.'

'Until we're picking up the television commercials from the Andromeda Galaxy,' suggested Derek.

I told you he had a vivid imagination.

12

Building the second receiver took another few weeks; Derek didn't manage to get away from the Prof's lab very much, but I had given up bothering with the radio telescope signals by now so I could spend about nine hours a day on this. Components became very short but the grant for cable had come through and I used this to buy transistors, coils, condensers etc from the local do-it-yourself radio shop. Derek turned on all his personal charm to borrow another long length of cable from the rather susceptible young woman in the telecommunications stores and I began the second long vigil of scanning the waveband.

This time there were much less electronic pyrotechnics so it wasn't such a strain on the eyes; it was just as tedious though, in fact more because most of the time there was just nothing, and by the end of term I'd got exactly nowhere.

While I was at home for Christmas I got the idea of taking a camp-bed back with me so that if I was too tired to go back to my digs after a session at the oscilloscope I could just spend the night in the lab. That led to misunderstandings though.

My mother has always had rather old-fashioned ideas and this talk about borrowing the camp-bed made her suspicious right away.

'You're sure you don't want it for one of those sit-ins or lie-ins or love-ins?' The trouble with my mother is that she watches too much television, and like all mothers she can never believe that a child of hers could ever be grown up.

'No Mum. It's strictly in the line of duty—for carrying out vital scientific observations.'

'You've got some fancy piece you're having it off with on the quiet.' The language that some parents use.

I assured her it wasn't that, though I must admit it did occur to me that if I ever got the chance to persuade Beryl along to the lab one evening I wouldn't pass up the opportunity. It was an intriguing thought and I wondered whether I dare invite her to come and see my oscilloscope, but after my disastrous experience of watching her television it seemed as if it would be asking for trouble. It wasn't as if there was anything to see.

Beryl was very nice to me when term started again. I used to see her for coffee every morning, and on Sunday evenings we used to have a fish and chip supper in the back room at Cappoccio's. She never invited me to her flat again and there never seemed to be a time when everybody was going to be out so that I could take her back to my digs. Mum had always said that when I found a girl I really cared for I should take her home for the weekend and introduce her to the family. I mentioned this to Beryl but she said she thought it might be a bit premature.

In the lab I was scanning the waveband from high to low frequencies, and it was about four-fifths of the way through that I began to get the signals, a very irregular frequency in the high audio range. It didn't appear to make any kind of sense so I just continued scanning down to the end of the band. There was this same signal all the way but since it was over such a large part of the waveband I assumed it must be some sort of interference.

I reported my progress or lack of progress to Professor Gannet who was paying a flying visit to the University during a brief interlude between a lecture tour in Ontario and a conference in Salzburg. He promised to find me an alternative project but agreed that I should make one final attempt to find some sense in the signals I had logged in the bottom end of the frequency-band.

Prof's conference left Derek free again and we looked at the signals together. We made a tape-recording of them and tried it through a speaker but nobody I played it to could make any sense out of it.

'The funny thing is that it has an absolutely constant amplitude while the frequency jumps about by a factor of two,' Derek pointed out.

That rang a bell somewhere, or do I mean a buzzer?

'Suppose we regard it as a constant frequency with some of the peaks just deleted?'

We tried that and it fitted.

'It's in Morse Code then,' said Derek, 'with a peak for a dash and a gap for a dot.'

I thought if there was anyone on Earth using that method of

14

transmitting Morse we would surely know about it and you couldn't get Morse code from space because no one there could have heard of Samuel Morse.

But there was something else. What had Prof said we'd got to look for? Messages in binary numbers. One for a peak and nought for a space.

'Copy them down, Derek.' I said excitedly.

The pattern was changing very rapidly but between us we managed to get quite a bit down.

'What do you think of these occasional half waves?' I asked.

'How about decimal points? suggested Derek, fired with inspiration.

The noughts and ones occurred mainly in groups of about twelve so we soon had a couple of pages full of binary numbers. Laboriously I began to change them to decimal.

One number occurred three times on the first page, 11·0010010001. I translated that first—three point one four one five nine.

'Eureka!'

I felt I should throw off my clothes and rush down the street, but it had been done before.

'Pi,' murmured Derek, but I could see he was disappointed.

'That is what we've been looking for,' I insisted. 'That is the most fundamental number in the whole of mathematics and it means there is intelligent life out there. Who knows how many years or centuries that message has taken to reach us?'

Derek was still disappointed. I think he'd been hoping for something more like, 'Hail Earthmen. Your fellow members of the Galactic Federation send their fraternal greetings.'

Professor Gannet was not disappointed though.

Chapter two

I still maintain that it wasn't my fault that the press got on to it the way they did. Admittedly I did send the cable to Professor Gannet and I can see now how the wording could be misinterpreted. 'Intelligible signals on screen from unidentified region of space.' But that was a fair description of what we'd observed wasn't it? Headlines like 'TV PROGRAMMES FROM OUR GALAXY WITHIN FIVE YEARS' and 'VIDEO LINK WITH PROXIMA CENTAURI' were pure invention, and I think the Prof was at least as much to blame as I was. He must have said something to the press when they intercepted him as he rushed out of the lecture and I think hiring a special plane exaggerated the importance of the whole affair.

Anyway next day the papers were full of it. All the front pages had banner headlines and most of the inside pages had articles by so-called experts reviving all the old discussions about life on other worlds. Several of the editorials contained long homilies stressing the importance of beginning relations with our new-found friends in space in an atmosphere of maximum cordiality and goodwill, and urging Mankind to put aside his petty little quarrels so that when, quite soon, the aliens began to visit us they would see the human race living in perfect harmony and tranquillity, not torn by international strife. Within hours my lab and office were knee-deep in reporters, cameramen, and special correspondents.

'Mr Brendon, can you tell us if television in the rest of the Galaxy is organized on a commercial or a public ownership basis?'

'Can you tell us which of the Earth's near neighbours are transmitting in colour and which ones are still at the old black and white stage?'

'Can you tell us if the 625 line standard is now general throughout the Galaxy?'

They had absolutely no idea. Professor Gannet kept well out of the way, steadfastly refusing to arrange a press conference and apart from forbidding me to say anything he left me to handle matters all by myself.

Of course they all wanted to see the receiver and the oscilloscope and by good fortune reception was excellent so I was able to give them a full demonstration of the low-frequency waves with the binary modulation but you never saw such a disappointed lot of men. Some of them turned quite nasty and made out that I'd dragged them all the way up from London on false pretences; one even suggested I ought to pay his fare. I told them about mathematics being a universal language and I explained about the fundamental importance of pi but I don't think they understood. The only evidence I had that any of them were listening at all was the headline in one paper the next day, 'TV LINK-UP JUST PI IN THE SKY.'

Most of the editorials that day mentioned irresponsible student hoaxes and discussed whether the vast amounts of public money being spent on the universities would not be better employed building another thousand miles of motorway or a fourth airport for London. One extreme left-wing paper did continue to take the matter seriously but the editor of that was mainly concerned to know what assurance the government could give that there would be no discrimination against green-faced aliens on the grounds of colour and that no repressive immigration controls would be enforced if visitors from other planets wished to take up residence here. The subsequent student demonstration in which a leading Conservative politician's car was overturned was organized entirely by a reporter from this paper.

So one way and another it was a week or two before the furore died down. I spent most of my time making careful records of the signals coming in but I couldn't make head or tail of most of them. Pi continued to crop up and about half the signals seemed to be numbers of some kind but the rest was just gibberish. Professor Gannet spent a lot of time poring over the records himself but even he couldn't decipher any of it.

I was puzzled to know how the signal came to be carried on such a wide range of frequencies, and Derek suggested we try

17

and sort it out by moving the aerials round, so he went out to the edge of the field while I stayed to watch the effect on the screen. Nothing he did seemed to make much difference though, and eventually he came back with one of the dipoles in his hand.

'It's come adrift I'm afraid,' he said, 'and there's another thing—the earth from the co-ax cables has broken.'

I don't know whether he realized the significance of that, but I did.

'Derek,' I said, 'how long will it take to modify this to receive very long waves, in the VLF band?'

'Three to thirty K/c, that's a bit low, but there's that old naval set, so if you just want a lash-up about half an hour I suppose.'

We lashed it up, switched on, and there was the old familiar signal.

'Well stone the crows. How did you work that one out?'

'The cable was acting as an aerial, picking up the low frequency direct.'

'Because it wasn't earthed.'

'It still leaves one or two problems though, doesn't it?'

'Such as?' he enquired.

'Such as how does a signal on that frequency get through the ionosphere.'

'I can answer that. It's a beat frequency between two hfs. Funny way to send a message though, isn't it?'

We left it at that for the time being. If I'd given the subject a bit more thought I might have realized then that the real explanation was something totally different.

I hadn't seen much of Beryl all this time, except at morning coffee, and then at last events began to take the turn I had been waiting for.

'Fred, Clive and I are thinking of forming an all male drinking club to meet at the "White Lion" every Wednesday night,' said Andrew Saltburn as I was sitting at breakfast with him one morning. 'Would you like to join?'

Fred, Clive, and Andrew were the three others in my digs, and what made Andrew's remark so interesting to me was the fact that Wednesday was Mrs Rowland's bingo night. A vista of exciting possibilities flashed through my mind.

'I don't think so, thanks Andy. I'm a bit too hard up this week.'

'We shall have a kitty to buy the beer so it won't come too heavy but still, please yourself. If you do decide to come we shall be in the bar from seven o'clock onwards.'

I could hardly wait till morning coffee time. Beryl was as warm and friendly as ever.

'Hello Harold. You look like that cat that swallowed the canary.'

'How would you like to come and sample my Spaghetti Bolognese?' I blurted out. 'Only out of a tin of course.'

'Well you are getting domesticated. But that would be smashing. I'm an absolute pushover for Spaghetti Bolognese. When would you like me to come?'

'This Wednesday,' I almost shouted.

'Oh dear, what a pity. I go out with Joan and Chloe every Wednesday but perhaps we could fix up some other day.' She really did look genuinely sorry.

'It has to be Wednesday,' I said bitterly. 'That's the only day. Couldn't you put off Joan and Chloe just this once?'

'It wouldn't be fair would it? I wouldn't like to let them down and it's a regular arrangement you see.' Her big brown eyes looked into my face with so much sincerity that I felt honoured to know someone with such high principles.

I saw Andrew in the common-room later that day.

'I think I shall be able to get along to the "White Lion" on Wednesday,' I said.

'Well that's great. It's the more the merrier for a thing like that isn't it?'

Fred, Clive and Andrew were all in the Physics Department, research students like me, only working in more conventional fields. They'd brought along five of the others out of that department so it made nine of us altogether, and as it was the inaugural meeting of the club the first thing we had to do, after we'd ordered a round of drinks, was to draw up a set of rules.

No soft drinks were to be allowed, no half pints, and no

women. There were to be a chairman, a vice-chairman, a secretary, that was Clive, a treasurer, and five committee members. Fred had brought a mallet to call the meeting to order so we elected him chairman and Clive had got a large notebook to write the minutes in. It was agreed that there must always be at least one round of drinks before each new item on the agenda.

I remember we started off very formally.

'The meeting is now open for nominations for the post of treasurer.'

'The next item on the agenda is etc etc.'

But things gradually got more disorganized and I don't think anyone can remember how the fight started or even who was fighting, but I can remember hearing the landlord's voice.

'Come on then you lot, out you go. We're not having that sort of thing here.'

'The meeting is adjourned to the "Fox and Hounds",' said Fred with great presence of mind, and we all trooped out, encouraged by two large bouncers who had appeared from behind the bar.

I should have turned right for the 'Fox and Hounds' but I think I must have turned left because I soon realized the others weren't there. I felt very sick at first but after I'd brought it all up on a bit of waste ground it didn't bother me any more. It was very difficult to concentrate on which way to go though.

I think I could walk fairly steadily, and I began to make my way along the side of the zoological gardens. These are in the park, next to the university campus, and I knew I was on the right road for my digs, so I decided not to bother with the 'Fox and Hounds.'

It was just by the main gate of the park that I saw the three girls coming towards me, all side by side with their arms linked, and naturally I stepped into the roadway to let them pass, but I think the pavement must have been cracked because I stumbled and lost my balance.

'It's Harold Brendon isn't it?'

'Harold darling, are you all right?'

Gently Beryl helped me to my feet and brushed the gravel

20

from my coat. How unjust I'd been to doubt her word when she said she was going out with her room-mates.

'Look Chloe, you and Joan go on. I'll walk back with Harold.'

I was about to protest that I'd be all right, but there was no point in refusing Beryl's help when her presence was always such a delight, and so we set off slowly arm in arm.

'I'm sorry to be a nuisance, Beryl,' I said apologetically.

'It's all right, Harold sweetheart. You bring out the best in me. Most girls have a Florence Nightingale hiding away somewhere in a corner of their hard little gold-digger's heart. We're all looking for an opportunity to be a ministering angel.'

I managed to find the key in one of my pockets, and Beryl opened the front door for me, then helped me into the sitting-room I shared with Fred, Clive, and Andrew. I remember sitting down in the big old arm-chair, and I think I asked Beryl if she'd like some supper. I can't remember whether she said she would or not, in fact I can't really remember anything after that.

When I woke up the sunlight was streaming through the gap in my bedroom curtains. The inside of my mouth felt like well-used glass paper, and there was a dull hammering in my fore-head. Gradually I fought through the fog in my brain to try and orientate myself. The alarm clock said half past seven, the time it was always set for, so it must have just woken me up, and propped up against it was a white envelope with 'Harold' written on the front. I opened it, took out the single sheet of paper, and read 'Darling, Hope you're feeling fit and bright this morning. If not I should try a cup of coffee and two aspirins. I'll see you in the Union Building when you come in. Your ever-loving Beryl. PS. Sorry I couldn't find your pyjamas but I don't think you'd be cold—I tucked you in well. B.'

That was it. That was what seemed unusual. Under the bedclothes I was stark naked. Oh the mortification. I knew I'd never look Beryl in the face again. And the opportunity I must have missed, with Beryl in my bedroom. For a moment I began to wonder seriously whether there might be something wrong with me. Was it some sort of Freudian defence mechanism that was always going to make me fall asleep whenever things

21

reached a critical stage? But perhaps I hadn't missed that opportunity. I just couldn't remember anything. I somehow dressed and groped my way downstairs.

Fred was spreading thick marmalade on his toast. The skeletons of two kippers lay on a dirty plate beside him. Andrew was just starting on a large bowl of porridge, and Clive was hungrily gulping at a huge mug of creamy chocolate. I wondered whether it had been three other people that I was drinking with last night.

'Hello Harold. What happened to you last night? I didn't see you at the "Fox and Hounds".'

'You should have been there. There's a little red-headed barmaid and honestly her dress only comes up to here, and the skirt only comes down to here.'

I reminded Clive that the rules of our new club specifically forbad the presence of women at a meeting.

'Oh barmaids don't count. But what's the matter with you? Have you got a hangover? I'm not surprised. The beer was terrible wasn't it?'

I didn't go down to the Union Building because I was too embarrassed, and I'd decided to make a cup of tea in the lab. I'd got quite a lot to do as a matter of fact because the Prof had recently agreed that I could have a 35 mm camera to record the signals, and it had only arrived the day before. I'd chosen a half-frame model with motor drive because the signals changed so rapidly that if I stopped to wind on by hand I was liable to miss something, but I hadn't much idea what exposure was required and I wasn't certain about the relationship between the shutter speed on the camera, and the time-base on the oscilloscope, so I was pretty busy up until eleven o'clock. Then there was a knock on the door.

'Harold. Harold. Are you there?' It was Beryl.

I let her in and she flung herself into my arms but I'm afraid I didn't respond. Prof was always liable to pop in at that time in the morning, and there's nothing inhibits my ardour more than that sort of possibility.

'Why didn't you come down to refec, Harold? I was so worried about you. Come down and have a cup of coffee now.'

I ordered black coffee, but it was really only a precaution because I was completely recovered by then, and we sat on our own at one of the tables by the window.

'I'm sorry I made such a fool of myself, last night, Beryl.'

'Oh that's all right. Don't worry about that. I thought it was rather sweet really.'

Rather sweet? What did she mean by that? Tactfully I enquired.

'Well getting drunk just because I wouldn't come to supper with you. I thought it was rather a compliment in a way, like joining the Foreign Legion, only not so irrevocable.'

'Anyway thank you for the ministering angel stuff.'

'I enjoyed it. And I really will come and have some supper one day.'

'It has to be a Wednesday, I'm afraid,' I explained.

'Well I'll let you know when I've got a free Wednesday. But now tell me what's the latest on the interstellar communication front.'

I brought her up to date and she listened with real interest. It's not often you get a combination of brains and beauty like that. Apart from Derek and Professor Gannet almost everybody thought my research project was a joke, but being a mathematician, of course, Beryl could appreciate the fundamental significance of pi, and realized that it was clear evidence that the signals came from some being with a mathematical intelligence.

'We couldn't get a signal like that just by chance could we?' I said.

'Surely not. Anyway you've had this over and over again haven't you? I'll work out the statistical significance if you like. But you know I've never actually seen this on your screen.'

'Well come and let me give you a demonstration. You could come this afternoon but it's very much better at night.'

The sudden thought of Beryl and that camp bed took my breath away. I knew I wouldn't be inhibited in the lab at night and I couldn't see Beryl being inhibited anywhere if only I could get her on her own. But I wasn't just making it up; the signals were very much clearer in the evening. During the day there was quite a lot of sporadic interference of some kind but as soon as people started to go home the background quietened down and the signals came over loud and clear. Of course when we realized the true nature of the waves we were picking up it was obvious why this was.

Beryl thought for a moment 'I mustn't be late back but if you could make it say seven thirty.'

'Tonight?' I said excitedly, hardly able to believe my ears.

'Will tonight be all right?'

The rest of our conversation came through to me in a sort of rose-coloured daze but I can remember arranging to pick Beryl up from her flat. Then I left to go back to the lab, and Beryl went off to a lecture on quantum mechanics.

I worked with the camera all the afternoon but I couldn't keep my mind on the job and I still hadn't sorted out the shutter speed when it was time for me to go back for my evening meal at Mrs Rowlands'.

It was a warm evening, and Beryl looked delicious in her thin summer dress. I felt very conscious about not having a car, and I asked Beryl if she'd like a taxi, which I couldn't really afford.

'Of course not. It's only ten minutes walk. Come on. Hold my hand.'

'We'll go through the park then, shall we?'

Under the trees round the lake pairs of bodies lay side by side and I wondered if it might give Beryl ideas; I had ideas already.

We turned in the gate and I unlocked the door of the lab. I had arranged the camp bed in front of the oscilloscope, so that we could sit side by side to look at signals, and I'd borrowed two cushions from Mrs Rowlands' sitting room.

'You just sit here while I adjust the tuning.'

As usual in the evening reception was very good, so I was able to hold the patterns steady while Beryl and I sat and watched, and she made rapid notes on a pad she'd brought. Within five or ten minutes pi had cropped up three times.

'It must be significant,' she agreed. 'But what's all this other stuff? Some of it's numbers, almost as if it's some kind of calculation.'

'I can't make head or tail of it.'

'You ought to keep as full a record of it as you can though for when you do manage to decipher it. Is that what the camera's for?'

I showed her all the photographic set-up, and she was quite impressed. I took a few shots of Beryl sitting and watching the screen and then some head and shoulder views just sitting and smiling. I let the window blind up for these and the sun slanted in through the window, making a sort of halo round her head. Afterwards I pulled the blind down again so that we could see the screen better and so no one could look in on us. The signals had stopped by then and I was going to switch off, but Beryl wouldn't let me.

'There might be some more in a minute, mightn't there?'

That meant she was going to stay awhile at least: I led her back to the camp bed, where she settled in relaxed luxury.

'What a lovely idea, being able to make yourself so comfortable on the job. Now if only we'd got a radiogram playing soft music.'

I could have brought my portable radio only I hadn't thought of it. I wondered whether to nip out for half a bottle of gin from the off-licence in Park Road but it would have broken the spell. I was doing all right as it was.

'Come and sit beside me, Harold darling, while we wait to see if anything else comes over.'

I was already on my way, but the invitation was an encouraging sign. I put both cushions behind Beryl and sat down beside her. She turned her face towards me and her warm brown eyes looked into mine.

'You know, Harold, I think you're very clever doing all this. When you started I thought it was a crazy idea.'

'So did I,' I confessed.

'But it isn't, is it? It's brilliant. And it's a great mystery.'

I gently pressed her shoulders back on the cushion, and covered her mouth with mine. I'd never met anyone who kissed with the tongue like that before. My chest was pounding as we stopped for breath.

'I love you Beryl.'

'You're trying to seduce me, aren't you?'

'Would you mind very much?'

She didn't answer and I felt very excited. I read in a book once that when a girl says no she means maybe, and when she says maybe she means yes. No answer counted as maybe, didn't it?

I kissed her again and then gently slid my hand between us. She closed her eyes and sighed lovingly as I began to undo the buttons down the front of her dress. Then she opened one eye and looked over my shoulder.

'Harold. Harold. Look. They've come back.'

She jumped up and I turned to look at the screen, which was once more a mass of signals.

Beryl sat on the bed with her dress unbuttoned to the waist, scribbling furiously in her notebook, and getting more and more excited as the rapid progression of modulated waves moved across the screen.

'What is it?' I asked.

'Look! 10.1011011111. There it is again. And again 10.1011011111. Four times in a minute. That can't be chance. You see what sort of calculations they are.'

I didn't get it. 'What is 10.1011 etc etc?' I asked.

'E of course.'

'E?'

'Exponential e, the base of natural logarithms, 2.7183.'

'What sort of calculations are they then?'

'Well I can't sort it all out, but I'm pretty sure that your chum in the Andromeda Galaxy is solving an extremely complex differential equation.'

'I don't think we could be getting signals from that far. It's more likely a planet belonging to one of the nearer stars.'

'Well anyway your friend in space, wherever he is. He's doing some pretty fancy integration I'd say. He's a better mathematician than I am.'

'Are you pulling my leg?' A sudden unworthy suspicion had entered my mind.

'No. It's true. Whoever is sending that stuff out must think Homo Sapiens is a bit brighter than he really is. Unless it's not meant for us at all. Yes that's it. Perhaps we're overhearing a message intended for someone else.'

'You are pulling my leg.'

'No. Honestly. Cross my heart.' She pressed a slim hand on her lace-covered bosom.

'Would that I were a glove,' I muttered.

'I beg your pardon.'

'Shakespeare. Romeo and Juliet. "See how she rests her cheek upon her hand. Would that I were a glove upon that hand, that I might touch that cheek".'

Beryl laughed, flattered I could see.

'Never mind that now, there'll be time for that later. We've got to get all these numbers down, then I can try and sort them out tomorrow.'

I tried to help copy down the signals, but Beryl was so quick at it that she and our unknown friend left me standing. She'd filled about sixteen pages before the patterns finally subsided to leave just a plain unmodulated wave.

'Don't they play the national anthem before they close down?' asked Beryl.

'No,' I laughed, 'but once that steady wave starts there's never any more until the next day. Joe must be having an early night tonight.'

'Well he's given us enough to be getting on with. I'll look at it tomorrow.'

Then she shut her notebook, the dear girl, and sat demurely while I rushed to turn the receiver off.

She put out her arms to receive me and we fell back on the bed in a clinging mass of fondness and desire. I kissed her neck, her ears, and her mouth. Our hands caressed and I knew it was going to be all right. But I knew I mustn't rush things. The night was young, and impatience would spoil everything.

I was aware of a wriggling from the delicious bundle of softness in my arms. It didn't seem like a fresh manifestation of passion although I wasn't sure.

'Are you all right Beryl darling?'

'Yes love. Just trying to look at my watch.'

'Oh it's only ten to nine.'

'I've got to go at nine.'

I looked at her aghast. 'At nine?'

'I'm meeting Paul Wheatline in the coffee bar at 9-30 and I

27

must go back and change first. This dress is a shambles, and look at my hair.'

I couldn't believe it. I almost wept. 'Beryl my darling! Don't go now Beryl.'

'I'm sorry Harold sweet, but I must go.'

'Stand him up,' I implored her, 'just this once, and tell him you were ill.'

Beryl was shocked. Her sad wide-open eyes looked so serious. 'You know I couldn't do that, Harold. I'm not that sort of girl.'

'Who's Paul Wheatline anyway?' I demanded.

'He's a very sweet boy who takes me out once a week and I'm very fond of him.'

'What about me?'

'I'm very fond of you too, Harold. That's why I asked Paul specially if we could make it later this evening so I could come here first and he was very understanding.'

I felt shot to pieces. 'Don't you find your love-life terribly complicated?' I asked bitterly.

'Not really,' she explained. 'I'm very conscientious you know, and as soon as I make a date I write it down very carefully in my diary, so as not to forget.'

'I thought you loved me.'

'I do love you, Harold. I think you're a dear sweet boy and I love you very much.'

'What about this Wheatline character then? Do you love him too?'

'But of course, Harold darling. You can love more than one person you know.'

'Not properly you couldn't. Not really.'

'Well my mother had five children and I know she loves all of us.'

'That's different.'

'No it isn't.'

'Why didn't you tell me about all these others?' I demanded.

'It's only four, and I thought you knew. Anyway to tell you the absolutely honest truth I wasn't really expecting you to be staying on after you got your degree.'

'Well I am sorry to upset your plans,' I said bitterly.

'Don't be like that, Harold, please. I'm ever so glad you did stay and I should have missed you terribly if you'd left.'

Suddenly blinkers seemed to fall from my eyes. One moment I was looking at the most beautiful girl I'd ever known, and the next minute there was just this stupid little tramp standing in front of me. I was very polite and controlled though.

'I think it would be better if we didn't see each other again, Beryl. I'll just lock up and walk back to the flat with you.'

But she didn't wait; without a word she slipped out of the door and ran across the grass.

Andrew was making himself a cup of cocoa when I got back to Mrs Rowlands'.

'Working late again then?' he said cheerfully. 'Any more messages from the little green men?'

'Only a picture postcard from Venus.'

'Well it takes all sorts I suppose. Want a cup of cocoa?'

We sipped the hot gritty black liquid in silence. There never seemed to be any milk left.

'Do you know Paul Wheatline?' I asked Andrew, apropos of nothing.

'Yes. He's a pharmacist. Goes out with that poxy little bag Beryl Candy. What is it they call her? Randy Candy.'

I punched him straight on the nose. I don't know why, because Beryl was nothing to me, but it was just sort of automatic. Andrew took it very well and that was lucky because he could give me a couple of stone in weight and a good four inches in reach.

'I'm sorry. I forgot she was a friend of yours too, but you didn't need to do that you know.' Andrew rubbed his nose.

'Why did you call her that?'

'It wasn't a very nice thing to say, I admit, but they reckon she's the easiest lay in the college. Have you been having a dabble?'

'No of course not. But what did you mean by poxy?'

'Clive saw her coming out of the clinic last term so she must have had a touch of something I suppose. I shouldn't worry though—she must be cured by now.'

I felt too sick to finish the cocoa so I just poured it down the sink and went up to bed. I didn't get to sleep for ages though; I was thinking about Beryl. She was a dear sweet affectionate girl and perhaps it was just that she had too much love for any one person. I thought it was very responsible of her to go to the clinic when she thought she might have caught something, and it was responsible of her to go on the pill as soon as she came up to college. I would have shared her with all the others but I knew it wasn't any good; she wasn't for me. I mourned for Beryl that night—not for the Beryl that was but for the girl I would have liked her to be.

It was at lunch-time next day that Chloe gave me the letter. There were three closely written sheets of foolscap and a sheet of Beryl's pale green scented notepaper.

'Dearest Harold,' I read, 'I feel pretty sure you don't want to see me any more and I can't really blame you, but I am sorry about last night, truly I am.

'As you see, I've transposed all the figures I copied down. I showed them to Dr Wendale at the maths lecture this morning and he says that as far as he knows it's an entirely original method of solving this type of differential equation. He considers it's brilliant, and at the moment he's under the impression that I did it myself. It seemed too complicated to explain about your messages from outer space.

'Anyway I hope they'll be useful for the thesis and in case I don't see much of you in the future the very best of luck.

All my love, Beryl.'

Sweet Beryl, she must have been up all night sorting out those calculations. For a moment I wanted to rush out into the corridor, looking for her everywhere to tell her I did want to see her again, as often as I could. But it was no good was it?

Idly I turned her letter over, and on the back there was a postscript.

'PS. Why don't you send a message back—not to me of course, I mean to Andromeda or Sirius or wherever it is.'

The funny part of it was that Professor Gannet suggested exactly the same thing.

Chapter three

Sending a message back was easier said than done. For one thing it meant building a transmitter and there was a lot of work involved in that, but I must say that Professor Gannet was very helpful.

'You may need a bit of technical assistance at this stage, Brendon, so I've arranged for my assistant, Derek Sandgate, to come down and give you a hand one afternoon a week. He's very busy but he says he thinks he could manage that, and although he's not exactly a theoretical genius I think you'll find him reasonably competent as long as you tell him exactly what to do.'

Actually Derek told me exactly what to do, which was just as well because the technical side of things was getting somewhat beyond me. He managed to slip down rather more than one afternoon a week and, in fact, I often wondered whether any of the Prof's work got done at all.

'Oh that's all right,' said Derek airily. 'I just spend a couple of hours on Monday morning lashing a few circuits together and it keeps him happy all the week.'

Professor Gannet was even more impressed with the news about e than he had been about pi, and he began coming down to see how the transmitter was progressing more and more often. I had begun a life of monastic dedication to interstellar communication, and the freedom from emotional entanglements left me plenty of time to concentrate on the project, or perhaps it was that pressure of work kept me from having time to fret about Beryl. Prof had persuaded a local electronics firm to give us a research grant of £5000 for the transmitter, but what they got out of it I couldn't see, except that we bought some of the bits and pieces from them.

So one way and another we were ready to go on the air within about four or five weeks. We even had a broadcasting licence, rushed through specially with a few wires pulled by the

Vice-chancellor, but I still hadn't a clue what we were going to broadcast. We didn't know which HF wavelengths to use of course and in the end we just used the low frequency as it was, although I didn't see how it was going to get through the ionic layers. I ought to have used my loaf over that, but I was too busy worrying about what sort of message we were going to send.

'They won't understand English, will they?' I pointed out to the Prof.

I thought he was going to blow his top at that. 'Brendon! Are you a complete imbecile? Surely you must have got the idea by now. We send them a message in mathematics.'

'Yes sir,' I apologized. But I still didn't see what we could say in mathematics. Admittedly they'd told us pi and e but just offhand I couldn't think of any more fundamental numbers like that. I wanted to ask Prof for more details but I thought I'd better not.

'I'll try and work something out,' I said.

'You do that Brendon, and don't make it too childish will you? Those chaps whoever they are appear to be pretty bright.'

'Yes sir.'

'I'll look in again in the morning, and you can tell me what you've decided on.'

Before I could say anything else he'd gone.

I sat at my desk with a pencil and a blank sheet of paper, hoping for inspiration. The message was going to take years or even centuries to reach its destination so it ought to be something worthwhile. I toyed with the idea of Pythagoras; they obviously wouldn't have heard of an old Greek character of course but they might know about the square on the hypotenuse. I couldn't think of a way to put it over though. If only I'd still been friends with Beryl, I was sure she'd have been bursting with ideas for mathematical messages. I was still pondering when Derek looked in.

'How's the pirate radio station then?' he asked cheerfully.

'We're not a pirate, we've got a proper GPO licence, and our own call-sign.'

'Yes I know, but that's the sort of thing they give radio hams with a range of about fifty miles, not a couple of hundred light years.'

'Well it's all in Prof Gannet's name, so he'll be the one they lock up, not me.'

'Anyway have you signed up a good disc-jockey yet? Plenty of heavy beat music, that's what you want. I'll lend you some of my old LPs if you like.'

'We've got to send a message in mathematics, something they can recognize as being absolutely fundamental.'

'How about 36 – 24 – 36?'

'What's that?' I asked naively. You can see what a state I was in.

'Last year's Miss Universe's vital statistics. That's pretty fundamental isn't it?'

'I'm afraid not. They won't be working in inches will they? And in any case their girls might not be the same shape as ours.'

'Really? No kidding?' Derek was obviously astounded at this novel suggestion. 'You mean they might be 24 – 36 – 24?'

'I know at least one girl around here who's not far off that.'

Derek was lost in thought for some time. I assumed he was trying to imagine what Miss Proxima Centauri would look like in a bikini, but I was wrong.

'I've got it,' said Derek. 'That's it. That's what you want to send, a list of prime numbers.'

'Prime numbers?'

'Yes. Numbers that are prime on earth are prime on any other planet, and in any other system of numerology. Old six-eyed Sidney out there will recognize at once that they're special numbers picked out by some highly developed intelligence.'

'Though you say it yourself. But you're quite right. That's exactly what we need. We can start at the bottom and work our way up. I'll suggest it to Professor Gannet next time he comes in.'

'Suggest it to old Gannet?' said Derek scornfully. 'You don't want to bother with him. We're all ready to go on the air, aren't we? What's wrong with now? This is Earth Station One calling the Universe. This is Earth Station One.'

'It's not Earth Station One, it's G4-KTV but there's no reason why we shouldn't start now I suppose. I think I know all the prime numbers up to a hundred, but we shall have to convert them to binary.'

We'd got the transmitter set up to send out a steady wave, with an interrupter device so that we could delete peaks as required, and this gave the same sort of morse code effect that our unknown correspondent used to send us the binary numbers.

'I'll switch on then shall I?' said Derek, doing so without waiting for an answer. 'You convert the primes to binary, and I'll start pushing them out.'

Laboriously I began working them out, passing them to Derek as I did so.

'Two=10, three=11, five=101, seven=111, eleven= 1011, thirteen=1101.'

As I passed each number to Derek he sent it off and then sat waiting for the next one. We'd got up to thirty-one when I noticed that Derek had switched the receiver on with the transmitter. Our signals were saturating it, the screen was just a mass of green light.

'Stop,' I shouted. 'You'll blow it up.'

Admittedly there was an automatic gain control, but the thought of a receiver designed to pick up faint signals from outer space being blasted by a powerful transmission on the same wavelength, right on its own doorstep, made my heart bleed. You get that sympathetic feeling for electronic equipment you know.

Derek stopped transmitting and the green glow faded from the oscilloscope, leaving the now familiar waves of the signal frequency. There were some very simple binary numbers coming over now.

'10, 11, 101, 111, 1011. . . .'

'Derek. Look,' I called in amazement.

'It's an echo,' he suggested. 'It must be bouncing off one of the planets.'

The numbers seemed to be coming back somewhat faster

than we'd sent them out, without the agonizing pauses while I did the working out. They very quickly got up to thirty-one, but then they didn't stop. They didn't stop. They didn't stop.

11111＝thirty-one, 100101＝thirty-seven, 101001＝forty-one, 101011＝forty-three, 101111＝forty-seven. . . .

Derek and I stared at the screen as the numbers steadily progressed. Within a minute they'd got to around the thousand mark, by which time I couldn't tell whether they were all prime or not.

'We've got an answer back,' said Derek.

'That's not many light years away,' I commented weakly, finding my voice again.

'It's some joker on the campus.'

I supposed it must be, but it was a joker who knew his prime numbers off better than I did.

'See if he can do square roots,' suggested Derek.

'Well let's try. Root two is 1·414 approximately.' I changed that to binary, and Derek sent it off.

Before you could do more than blink an eyelid the square roots of all the numbers up to 256 flashed across the screen, each one to twelve places in binary. At least I think they did, but to be strictly honest I only had time to recognize the easy ones like root four, root nine, and root sixteen etc.

But I was beginning to get the idea now. 'We'll see if he knows the Fibonacci series,' I suggested. This is a series in which each term is the sum of the two previous ones, so it goes 1, 1, 2, 3, 5, 8, 13, etc.

Anyway we sent off the first seven numbers just to see if Sidney Six Eyes recognized it, and he did. Offhand I'd say he must have known it somewhat better than Fibonacci did, because the next twenty-five terms flashed back without a moment's pause.

I was rather at a loss to know what to send next, and all Derek could suggest was 'Take me to your leader,' which didn't seem very appropriate.

However, our correspondent had got the bit between his teeth now, and I think he was trying us with a few problems of his own, but if so he was out of our league because I couldn't even read the questions, and nor could Derek. Then I suppose

35

he got discouraged, because he shut down and we didn't get another squeak out of him for the rest of the day.

Of course when Professor Gannet heard about all this he immediately assumed personal control, which would have upset me somewhat but for the fact that it was that day that my period of monastic dedication came to an abrupt end.

I was just on my way back to the lab after lunch when I saw this girl walking across the quadrangle. She was a very ordinary sort of girl and I'd never noticed her around before, but as we drew level she looked at me and smiled. She just smiled like you might to a person you know slightly, but it was as though something had hit me between the eyes.

I sat in the lab all the afternoon looking at the oscilloscope to see whether the signals had come back, but all I saw all the time was this girl smiling at me. It was a sort of sweet sad wistful smile and it made me feel as if I wanted to look after her.

Next morning Professor Gannet came in as usual and I told him about the prime numbers and the square roots and the Fibonacci series and how we were getting answers back by return of post.

'That means it's from our solar system, and only one of the planets is inhabited, that's for sure, so the messages come from Earth.' He had a very commonsense approach despite the bees in his bonnet.

'That means it's virtually certain to be a practical joker at the University,' he went on grimly, 'and when I find out who the moronic ape is I'll have his guts for garters.' He had a picturesque turn of phrase when roused, for a Prof.

'He's quite a bright mathematician,' I pointed out.

Prof was very impressed with the performance of this chap on the other end of the line, despite the doubts about his authenticity. I showed him how to transmit and he insisted on taking over. I don't know what he was sending out but he seemed to be getting answers back pretty smartly, and he was working like mad copying it all down. I think he'd forgotten I was there; he didn't even answer when I spoke to him, so I wandered off to the Union Building for a cup of coffee. There was someone I wanted to look out for.

I got my coffee and sat down at the table nearest to the counter, where I could see everyone coming in. Andrew and Clive turned up after a while, and then Fred with Sally West, a red-headed girl in the Education Department he was knocking about with at that time. The others were all talking about the rag magazine; I think Clive or somebody had sent in a joke and it had been rejected on the grounds that it wasn't near enough to the bone but I didn't really pay much attention. I was looking for a face with a smile.

Suddenly she came in the door at the back, on her own, wearing the same brown woollen dress she'd had on the day before. She walked straight past me without a glance, bought her cup of coffee, and then stood with it in her hand, looking all round as if she was hoping to see someone she knew. I wanted to jump up and tell her to come and sit by me, but I daren't, so I tried to will her to come and sit at our table. I know you won't believe it, but that's exactly what she did do.

She took three steps down the gangway until she was right level with me, and she was still looking round everywhere as if she didn't know a soul in the place. She wasn't looking at her cup of course, and it slid right out of the saucer, crash, on the floor beside my chair. There was coffee all over my shoes, and the poor girl didn't know what to say.

'Oh! Oh! Oh dear. Your shoes. And your trousers. I'm terribly sorry.'

She'd got a tiny little lace handkerchief, and do you know she bent down and started wiping the coffee off my shoes with it.

'Don't bother about that. It'll dry off all right. You sit here while I go and get you another cup.' I wasn't going to waste an opportunity like that was I?

She was still very upset when I came back with the fresh coffee. I fetched another chair and we squeezed into the space between Clive and Fred.

'I'm afraid it's ruined your shoes forever.'

'They're only old ones, so don't worry about that. Which department are you in?'

37

'I'm taking a teaching diploma.'

'You've got your degree then, have you?'

'Yes, in English. I want to specialize in teaching backward readers.'

'That's a funny thing to go in for.'

'I don't think so. I think it's very important and I'm sorry that you think it's funny.'

Trust me to say the wrong thing. 'I didn't mean it like that,' I apologized.

'You're the one that's been getting messages from outer space, aren't you?'

I was astonished. 'How did you know that?'

'Sally told me.'

'You know Sally West then do you?'

The two girls acknowledged one another, and we had introductions all round. The girl with the smile was called Alison Gold, she came from Shropshire, and was living in Southdown Hall, the women's hostel. We chatted for about twenty minutes about Shropshire and Clothcoats, and backward readers and communication satellites. Finally when we were the only two left at the table Alison went off to a lecture and I walked on a long carpet of super-pneumatic air all the way back to the lab. All the time I had to keep telling myself it was really true. I'd gone down to the refectory determined to look out for an unknown girl with a smile and now, purely because of that accident with the coffee, Alison and I were almost like old friends. I'd look out for her at coffee time tomorrow and go and sit beside her.

When I got back to the lab I found that Prof Gannet had fetched Professor Bedford from the Maths Department and the two of them were hard at it sending out abstruse calculations and getting the answers back at the speed of light. Gannet didn't seem to notice I was back, but Prof Bedford introduced himself.

'Good morning Brendon. I hope you don't mind us butting in on your project but these signals are absolutely fascinating. It was a brilliant piece of work spotting them in the first place.'

I was flattered at their interest and glad to be relieved of the responsibility for carrying on a mathematical conversation with an alien Einstein. Prof Bedford was full of ideas.

'We're thinking of sending the messages out in decimal now, with four binary digits to represent each decimal digit. It'll make things simpler for us if your friends out there can catch on to it.'

'Sidney Six Eyes will catch on all right,' I assured him. I didn't exactly understand what he was going to do myself, but I felt sure the unknown alien would.

So Prof Bedford started bashing out the messages; Gannet must have shown him how to transmit while I was talking to Alison. This time there was a distinct pause, about five seconds I'd say, while Sidney was working out what we were up to. Then his replies started coming back in an absolute torrent. You could almost feel his enthusiasm for the new system.

After that Prof Bedford sent out one of the papers from last year's honours maths exam. The time allowed was supposed to be three hours, but Sidney did it in one minute and fourteen seconds; I was timing him.

'If it is a practical joker it must be someone who took honours maths last year and can still remember the answers,' said Prof Bedford.

'Try him with this year's,' suggested Gannet. That hadn't been taken yet, of course.

Bedford sent out one of the papers he'd got planned for that summer, and the answers came back in one minute ten seconds.

'It is with considerable diffidence that I come to this conclusion,' announced Professor Bedford, 'because I have never believed in flying saucers myself, but I think we are forced to admit that we are not dealing with any human being but with a creature of markedly superior intelligence.'

'The problem is, where is he?' said Gannet. 'The answers come back in a matter of seconds, so it's not a question of outer space. The creature must have landed on Earth.'

'Why hasn't anything been seen then?'

'Perhaps he's in orbit.'

'My dear Gannet, are you seriously putting forward the hypothesis that an alien space-ship has come to the Earth and is at present orbiting round it, presumably in preparation for landing?'

'I know it sounds a bit way out, but what's your explanation?'

'I don't know,' Bedford confessed, 'but anyway if he's in orbit we should only be in contact for a few minutes each time, while he's above the horizon, unless there's more than one.'

I knew the answer to this; I'd been giving it some thought since we got the prime numbers back so promptly. 'Stationary orbit,' I murmured. 'They keep in phase with the rotation of the Earth, always over the same spot you see.'

'Yes thank you, Brendon, we have heard of stationary orbits.' I think Professor Gannet resented me getting to it before he did. One way and another I could see I was definitely beginning to be superfluous. When two profs get together they haven't much time for the ordinary intellectual hoi polloi, have they?

'If these aliens are about to land we ought to inform the Home Secretary or something you know Bedford.'

'They seem friendly enough though. I'm sure they can't mean us any harm, and if the press get hold of it we shall be trampled to death by reporters, cameramen, and TV commentators. It was bad enough when it was just pi, but now with an alien space-ship orbiting the Earth they'll go mad.' Professor Bedford's mind boggled noticeably.

'I think all the same,' Gannet went on, 'I will just drop a line to a chap I know in the Foreign Office. Just in case.'

They obviously weren't including me in the conversation so I quietly left and went to lunch. I was feeling pretty despondent, I must admit; the developments were exciting enough but I was obviously being elbowed out. I'd thought it might make a nice little Ph.D thesis; now it seemed more likely to form the basis of Professor Gannet's FRS.

I spent the afternoon playing bridge in the common-room. There didn't seem to be much point in going back to the lab while Gannet and Bedford were in residence and I thought that if I hung around the Union Building I might see Alison again. There was no sign of her by five though, so I gave it up and went back to Mrs Rowlands' to spend the evening watching television. And guess what was on—'Space Rangers', with Jet Columbus and his intrepid band of galactic explorers finding life on every planet they touched down on. There was a sexy-looking bird who lost more of her clothes every time she was captured by the alien monsters, and I was sure she was going to end up freezing to death, stark naked, but then this handsome space-captain rescued her and brought her back to Earth in the nick of time and a nice warm negligée. I wished Sidney could have seen it; it didn't look as if I was going to have much more to do with him though, now the top brass had moved in. However, Professor Gannet had other ideas.

I got into the department fairly early next morning, hoping at least to have half an hour on my own, but Prof was waiting for me.

'Ah Brendon, I've been looking for you. It's about the unidentified residue of these signals. Professor Bedford is sure it's not mathematical, and I think it must be speech.'

'Yes sir.' So where did I come in, I wondered. I soon found out.

'I've been talking to Dr Glazunov from the Department of Slavonic Languages, and he's agreed that if you can get a microphone and loudspeaker connected up he will try and converse with this alien.'

He's bonkers, I thought, or could it be that Prof was a Jet Columbus fan?

'I don't think they'll speak Russian, sir,' I suggested diffidently—Jet Columbus's aliens spoke pure Tennessee—but I could see I'd said the wrong thing again.

'Brendon, will you never get the idea? Dr Glazunov speaks fifteen languages, fourteen fluently, and he is a expert on linguistics. He will take the alien language apart and see how it is built up.'

And the best of luck, I thought, idly wondering which language it was that Dr Glazunov had so much difficulty with. Of course I found out as soon as I met him; it was English.

'I want you to get the necessary apparatus fitted up as quickly as possible,' went on Professor Gannet. 'Expense is no

41

object, and if you think high-fidelity equipment is necessary just order it.'

'Stereo?' I enquired, but Prof didn't notice the irony.

'Yes of course,' he said. 'Anyway I'll leave it to you, but don't forget it must be as soon as possible,' and he swept out of the door.

As you can imagine, this called for a conference with Derek right away, so I rang him up on the internal telephone and he came straight down.

'It's pretty simple really, isn't it?' he said. 'We just have to put in an extra stage to take the modulating frequency off the carrier wave and put it out through the loudspeaker. I don't know what sort of racket it'll be though.'

It took us just over a week to get the extra circuits finished, because as well as modifying the receiver we had to fit up the transmitter with a microphone and a stage to modulate the signal frequency with human speech.

I didn't see Alison at all for several days. I went down to the refectory every day and I would have liked to sit there all the morning waiting to see if she turned up, but Prof was badgering me so much about the transmitter that I couldn't spare more than ten minutes or so. Then on the Wednesday as I was hurrying through the swing doors I heard a bang and a cry behind me, and there was Alison on the floor. The poor girl! I'd let the heavy swing door go right back in her face, and I could have sworn there was nobody just behind me.

Fortunately she wasn't badly hurt but I felt terrible; I didn't know what to say.

'Alison! Alison! I didn't see you. Are you all right? Are you hurt? I'm sorry. I didn't know there was anyone there.'

'It's all right. It's nothing,' she said bravely, getting up and rubbing her knee. I was going to rub it for her but I thought I'd better not.

Anyway we went in together and I bought her a cup of coffee. We sat at the table by the window and talked a bit, then Alison said she'd have to get back to the Education Department. I walked all the way with her; she was still limping slightly and I could see she was rather shaken.

'I've only got one more lecture this morning, then I think I'll go back to Hall,' she said.

'I'll come and meet you then and walk up with you,' I promised.

One way and another I didn't get much work done on the transmitter that day, but Derek was managing all right without me. I still felt terrible about knocking Alison over with the door although I had to admit it had all turned out for the best, and it would have been silly to waste the opportunity wouldn't it?

I walked up to Southdown Hall with Alison at lunch time, and then I called again in the evening to see how she was getting on. By then she was fully recovered and we went for a walk in the park.

Did I tell you what Alison was like? She was about five feet five, quite slim, with short brown hair and brown eyes, and that kind of wistful smile I told you about. She wasn't really glamorous like Beryl, but she had something about her that sort of pulled at your heart. We walked all round the park holding hands and talking about absolutely everything you can imagine. Several times I almost suggested we should stop and sit down on the grass but somehow I never did. I felt this terrific protective instinct and right from the start I wanted her. I wanted her much more than I'd ever wanted Beryl. It was like a sort of compulsion.

We stayed in the park until it closed and then we strolled through the early spring evening back to the hall. I suggested we should call at the 'Golden Lion' for a drink but Alison didn't want to.

'I think I ought to have an early night, you know. Thank you very much for coming to see me, and I did enjoy the walk, Harold.'

'So did I, Alison. Anyway I'll come again tomorrow at the same time just to make sure you haven't had a relapse.'

'Do you think I might?'

'It's quite possible. With a case like this you just can't be too careful. I think I should come and see you every night for at least a week before we could definitely say you're out of the

43

wood.' I was really pushing my luck; I don't know how I had the nerve but it paid off.

'We don't want to take any chances,' she agreed. 'Same time tomorrow then. But I must go in now I'm afraid. Goodnight Harold.'

'Goodnight Alison.'

We stood looking at one another for a few seconds, then I put my hands on her shoulders and brought my face close to hers, slowly so she could stop me if she wanted to, but she didn't. We clung together in a long kiss for several minutes and then she slipped out of my arms and in the front door.

It was the day after that we taught the alien to play draughts. The circuits were almost finished except for the matching transformers we were still waiting for and Derek had come down for a chat, but there wasn't anything we could do on the set.

'We ought to send out one or two messages just to keep in touch and show him we're still friends,' suggested Derek.

'I've completely run out of ideas for mathematical messages,' I said.

'Why not see if he can play draughts?'

I thought about that; it was certainly an original idea, and there didn't seem to be any insuperable difficulties. It's conventional for draughts players to number all the squares on the board, of course, so that a move can be fully described merely by giving the numbers of the squares the piece starts from and lands on.

We had to describe the board first, but $8 \times 8 = 64$ took care of that, and we had to say which squares the pieces started on. Then we went straight into the first game. Sidney caught on at once—he really was bright—but I wiped the floor with him all the same.

'What about that then?' I said. 'How's that for a devastating bit of play?' I had taken the last three pieces in one go.

'You certainly beat him,' agreed Derek, 'but I wonder if there wasn't something we forgot to tell him. He had no way of knowing whether you had to take your opponent's pieces or get rid of your own, had he?'

44

'Nonsense. It's just that draughts is a game where experience counts for more than superficial cleverness. I'm the better player, that's the plain fact of the matter.'

'Have another game then—'

'It's your turn now.'

'No. You play him again.'

'All right. He's not really in my class though, is he?'

It was clear from the beginning of the second game that the alien had learnt a lot from his first attempt. He was giving nothing away this time, and we swapped piece for piece until we each had six left on the board. Then Sidney made a slip and I was one ahead. The next move he offered me another piece but I was suspicious straight away. I saw what would happen if I took it, but of course it was too late; I was obliged to take. Sidney's next move wiped out four of my pieces, and with four to two left on the board the rest of the game was just routine demolition, which didn't take very long at all.

'Hard luck,' said Derek sympathetically. 'I think he's got the idea now.'

He certainly had. That first game was the only one he ever lost, and in fact after one or two more we gave up trying. We thought of having a go at teaching him to play chess but without any way of sending speech we couldn't see how to explain about the different pieces.

Anyway as soon as the new transformers arrived Professor Gannet was down with Dr Glazunov for the official opening ceremony, and we had other things to think about.

With the audio stage working the mathematics came over as a series of clicks, but of course it was the other stuff we were interested in. Derek and I had a sneak preview, so we knew what to expect and I was watching Prof's face with great interest as he listened to Sidney's conversation for the first time. It was the most fascinating series of hoots, squeaks, gurgles, and whistles you could imagine, culminating in a gigantic raspberry and a noise like water running away. Prof looked puzzled at first, then angry.

'Is this supposed to be a joke Brendon? What do you mean by wasting my time and Dr Glazunov's? Are you trying to make a monkey out of me?'

45

'No sir.'

'Please what is making the monkey?' enquired Dr Glazunov.

'It really is genuine sir,' I assured Professor Gannet. 'That's really what's coming over.'

'Ridiculous. You've got it all wired up wrong.'

'The tone and sound quality depend on the receiver,' I admitted.

'Should we cut the treble and give it a bit more bass?' asked Derek.

We tried that and the result was even ruder. Prof appeared to be about to go into an apoplectic fit; I rushed to the set and cut the bass just in time to avoid a nasty accident.

With the treble and bass both cut the middle frequencies sounded relatively innocuous, and at any rate Prof seemed satisfied.

'Yes that's better Brendon. I told you it wasn't tuned in properly. Now Dr Glazunov, does that have any relation to one of the Slavonic languages? How does it strike you?'

Dr Glazunov leapt back in alarm. 'Who is going to strike me?'

'Do you know what he says?' asked Prof, speaking very slowly, as though to a small child. 'Can you un—der—stand?'

'He is not the Russian, not the Polish, and not the Croatian, but he may be the Welsh. I do not speak the Welsh.'

I think that Prof was beginning to lose confidence in the Head of the Slavonic Languages Department, but anyway before he went we did get him to say 'Hello. Good morning. Greetings from the Earth', in all his fourteen and a half languages, but none of them drew any response.

Professor Gannet wasn't going to let it go at that though. Within the next few days he combed the University and brought along to the lab an incredible variety of linguistic acquaintances who attempted to converse in French, German, Spanish, Italian, Portuguese, Arabic, Chinese, Japanese, Yiddish, Urdu, and Swahili. You name it and he tried it, but they were all a dead loss.

Meanwhile you'll be wondering how I was getting on with Alison, and the answer is not too badly at all. I'd been calling to see her every evening since the accident with the door and even in that short time it had got to be a habit for both of us. Not a habit in any derogatory sense, but more in the way of being an accepted part of life.

I never had to scheme to be alone with Alison; we were alone all the time, walking in the park, sitting in the back row at the cinema, or having tea or supper in her room, and all the time we talked. She didn't talk too much, like some girls, but she listened as well while I told her about what I wanted from life, what I hoped to do and to be, what I admired and what I hated—lots of things I'd never told anyone before. When we walked in the park I held her hand, when we sat in the cinema I put my arm round her waist, and when we said goodnight we clung together and kissed until we gasped for breath, but that was all.

I wanted Alison more than ever. It was agonizing and she was always inaccessible but she would say no so sweetly and charmingly that I couldn't be offended.

'It's very sweet of you Harold, and very flattering. I do appreciate it, honestly.'

As she gently removed my hand from her thigh she would kiss me harder than ever.

As I said, it was agonizing, but I wanted her so much that I didn't care how long I had to wait.

Alison had a wonderful sense of humour, and when I told her about Prof Gannet's attempts to translate the snorts and hoots into Russian and Japanese she nearly died laughing.

'He sounds an interesting character. I should rather like to meet him.'

'What, Professor Gannet?' I asked incredulously.

'No silly. Sidney Six Eyes.'

'Well that's easy. It's a bit late tonight; he usually goes off the air around nine, but I could take you down about half past seven tomorrow.'

At the thought of Alison and the camp bed my pulse rate gave an upward lurch, but it was an idle dream; I hadn't much hope that anything would come of it really.

'That would be wonderful. Are you sure no one would mind?'

'Oh no. I often have to work overtime,' I assured her.

So I collected Alison the next evening and we set off through the park. The sky was overcast when we started, and as we were passing the bandstand I felt a large drop of rain hit my cheek, then three more splattered on the path.

'We'd better shelter,' I said.

'No. Let's run for it.'

We ran for it, three hundred yards to the lab door, and by the time we got there we were soaked; water dripped from every corner of us.

'I'm sorry,' Alison apologized. 'I think your suggestion would have been better. Never mind, it's warm in here and we'll soon dry out.'

I took my sodden jacket off and hung it over a chair. Without blinking an eyelid Alison stripped down to two flimsy pieces of green nylon, deciding that as they were only slightly damp she could safely leave them on. It was torture, I can tell you, but worse was to come.

'You'd better get those wet trousers off,' she insisted, helping me unbuckle the belt. I did as I was told feeling that matters were out of my hands, then stood dazedly looking at Alison. I hadn't realized before just what a perfect shape she had.

'Aren't you going to switch on?'

'What? Oh! Yes. Would you like to see it on the screen or hear it on the loudspeaker?'

'I don't know. Which is best? Couldn't we have both?'

So we had both, first the oscilloscope and then the loudspeaker, but there wasn't a thing from either. I felt mortified, but Alison didn't seem to mind. Some girls would have accused you of dragging them along under false pretences to try and seduce them, but I don't think the thought ever entered Alison's head.

'Let's sit down and chat while we wait for something to come through,' she suggested.

So we sat and chatted. I told her how beautiful she was and she thanked me kindly. I put my arms round her, I kissed her, and she shuddered with delight, but when I made a tentative move towards one of the pieces of green nylon once again her hand gently removed mine.

'Alison my darling, I love you. . . .'

48

'I'm sorry Harold. You know that I love you too and I want you so much that I daren't let us go any further than we do, not yet sweetheart.'

You couldn't be angry with a girl like that, but like I said it was purgatory.

'Try the signals again,' she suggested.

So I switched on and there was Sidney in full swing. We looked at the mathematical signals on the oscilloscope but Alison wasn't really interested in that. Then we changed over to the loudspeaker and Alison listened enchanted.

'Can you understand it?' I asked rather fatuously.

'No of course not,' she laughed, 'but it's marvellous isn't it?'

'What do you mean?'

'Well listen to the range of sounds. If that is some kind of speech there must be at least fifteen vowels, and a good sixty to seventy consonants.'

'You should hear it with the bass and treble in.'

'Seriously though,' she went on, 'didn't you say that from his grasp of mathematics Sidney must be extremely intelligent?'

'You can say that again. He's definitely in the genius class in that subject.'

'In that case it's quite likely that his language is very much more complex than ours, and there's probably very little chance of a human being learning to understand it.'

'Yes I think that must be it. Prof has certainly given it a good run, but I'm afraid it's no go. There's really nothing we can do about it, is there?'

'Of course there is.'

'What?'

'You could teach him to speak English.'

I looked at her in astonishment.

'Couldn't you?' she went on.

The idea had never occurred to me and now that it did the answer was no.

'Would you like me to?' Alison said.

'You? How?'

'Teaching backward readers is my job, or it's going to be. Remember?'

'Sidney isn't backward.'

'No, but I should think he'll find English rather difficult at first, being so different from what he's been used to.'

'Yes,' I murmured weakly, 'you could be right.'

'Would you like me to start now? I haven't got any books with me, but I can remember a lot of it.'

I felt a complete sense of unreality. 'Why not?' I heard my voice answer.

'Well you just have a nice rest on the camp bed while I start him off on Book One.'

Chapter four

I'd fallen asleep again. It sounds terrible, I know, but I'd had a lot of late nights and some pretty hectic days and I'd been listening to Alison's elementary English lesson for hours. It was going on well after the time the signals usually stopped, and she was getting all sorts of hoots and gurgles in reply, so I suppose she must have aroused Sidney's interest to keep him up late, but it didn't sound to me as if she was getting any intelligible answers. Finally the sound of Alison's voice, sweet, loved though it was, had lulled me into complete unconsciousness.

'The dog is big. The cat is fat. The cat sits on the red mat. The big dog sees the fat cat. The cat is Tim. The dog has a pup.'

The last thing I remember was wondering how an alien from outer space could possibly be expected to know what a cat and a dog were.

When I woke up it was morning and Alison was snuggled up beside me on the camp bed.

'What's happened? Where are we?' It took me a minute to locate myself.

'Good morning,' said Alison. 'You slept well.'

'You've been here all night. What will they say at the hall?'

'That's all right. I signed out just in case,' she explained.

'Did you get anywhere with the English lesson?'

'Would you like a demonstration?'

I didn't know what she was going to demonstrate but I just waited while she switched on and took up the microphone.

'Hello. Are you there? This is Alison.'

There was no response so she tried again.

'Hello. This is Alison. Are you awake yet?'

Again there was no response at first, then suddenly the loudspeaker reverberated with a deep bass voice, harsh and mechanical, but easily understood.

'The cat sits on the mat. The man pats the dog. Hello Al—i—son.'

'What do you think of that?' she asked.

'The dog is Tom, the cat is Tim,' the alien added by way of explanation.

I didn't know what to say. It was incredible. I'd heard of people learning to teach English as a foreign language, but I felt sure they didn't do it this way.

'Tom sits in the sun,' boomed the loudspeaker. 'The bad dog runs after the fat cat.'

'Is that Book One?' I asked faintly.

'Yes, that is, but he's half-way through Book Three actually. Another two lessons and I shall have taught him all I can, so he'll have to go up to the next form. I only do backward readers, you know.'

I wondered whether I really was awake but everything seemed real enough, even the stiff pain where I'd been lying on the metal bar at the side of the camp bed.

'Have you asked him what his name is?'

'Yes. Would you like to hear?'

Alison handed me the microphone. 'You introduce yourself and then ask him what his name is.'

'Hello,' I said tentatively. 'My name is Harold. What is your name?'

So the alien told his name. It sounded like a hippopotamus's bath night.

'Yes I see what you mean. It'll be interesting to hear Prof's comments on that.'

'I'm hoping that when he's had a few more lessons he may be able to give us an anglicized version.'

'That would be helpful,' I agreed.

I walked back to Southdown Hall with Alison and then I just got back to Mrs Rowlands' in time for breakfast with Clive, Fred, and Andrew. I wanted to tell them all about the English lesson but I was afraid they might get the wrong idea, and I couldn't admit that I'd been asleep at the time, so I had to be a bit evasive.

'Still trying to break through the language barrier?'

enquired Fred. 'Have you thought of trying Liverpudlian?'
Actually he comes from the Wirral.

'Not quite. The latest plan is to teach them English.'

'Well it's the same thing.'

'I suppose you really have been working all night,' said
Clive, 'or have you been having it off with that new bird of
yours?'

'No of course not.' I could feel I was blushing and I hoped it
didn't show.

'He's going to have an uphill job there,' commented
Andrew. Andrew has a one-track mind, and he prides himself
on being able to size up any girl at a single glance. He says it
saves him a terrible lot of wasted dinners. I resented him
talking like that about Alison but I didn't say anything.

I went and changed my clothes, which although dry didn't
exactly look freshly valeted, then I went straight back to the
University. I wanted to make sure I could communicate with
Sidney on my own and then I thought I'd better report the
latest news to Prof straight away.

Sidney was in good voice again. 'Hello Harold,' he boomed.
'The quick brown fox jumps over the lazy dog.'

That must be from Book Three, I thought, unless Alison has
been teaching him typing. Anyway the communication
channel was obviously still open so I telephoned Prof's secretary and asked her to pass the news on to him.

He was down in the lab in about three minutes.

'What's all this now, Brendon? Margaret says you claim to
have been talking to the alien. Have you found out what
language he speaks then?'

'It's English sir,' I said, wondering what response that piece
of news would elicit.

'English? Balderdash! You've been imagining things. I'd
have noticed if he'd been speaking English.'

'I have a friend in the Education Department and she
taught him sir. Would you like to hear?'

'I suppose we'd better clear this nonsense up. Go on then,'
he said ungraciously.

I picked up the mike. 'Hello. This is Harold Brendon. Are
you there? I have brought Professor Gannet to meet you.'

53

'Hello Harold. The cat sat on the mat. Tom the dog has a bone.'

I heard Prof draw his breath in. His face went red then purple and I thought he was going to burst something.

'Brendon,' he shouted, 'I've told you about this before. That sense of humour of yours will get you into serious trouble one of these days. Are you under the impression that today is April the First or something?'

Hurriedly I seized the mike again. 'Hello,' I said. 'Professor Gannet does not like cats and dogs. Say good morning to him please.'

'Good morning Professor Gannet,' boomed the loudspeaker. 'I am very pleased to meet you.' Alison's lessons had evidently gone further than I realized.

Prof gradually calmed down. 'Yes,' he conceded, 'I must admit that's a significant breakthrough.'

Professor Gannet spent some time in the lab talking with the alien, and of course he didn't bother with the Book One cat on the mat stuff.

'Please tell me your estimated position, your height above sea level, and orbital velocity. What method of propulsion do you use? Please inform me of the power of your transmitter in kilowatts.'

Unfortunately I don't think Sidney understood a thing he said. Over and over again the loudspeaker reverberated with a deep-throated plea for enlightenment.

'Would you please explain in more simple words. I am very sorry but I do not understand. Please explain. Please repeat that.'

Professor Gannet had no patience with this sort of thing as you can imagine. 'I thought this alien of yours was supposed to be a genius, but he sounds pretty moronic to me. Can't you teach him to understand simple English?'

'It's his vocabulary,' I explained.

'Please, I need more words,' boomed Sidney, as if to back me up.

'Well that's no problem,' said Prof decisively. 'Brendon, run and fetch the Shorter Oxford Dictionary from the library will you.'

I fetched both volumes at the double, panting somewhat over the last fifty yards.

'Now,' said Prof, 'you just sit here at this desk and read it out to him.'

'What all of it?'

'Yes. It's no good messing about until he knows what we're talking about, is it?'

'It'll take weeks,' I groaned.

'Well you'd better start straight away then.'

There's no doubt about it that Professor Gannet has determination and drive; when someone else is doing the work there is absolutely no stopping him. As soon as he had me sitting down at that desk reading out the words and their meanings he was off to attend to one of the other irons in his fire.

I ploughed on from aardvark to abigail, from acacia to advocate, marvelling how many words I'd never heard of and wondering how Sidney could possibly remember them all. Once or twice I stopped to ask how he was getting on and each time he assured me he was fine.

'Yes thank you Harold. I shall remember all these words. They will be very useful.'

I remember I'd got up to alpenhorn by lunch-time, then I had three-quarters of an hour rest. When I got back to the lab Derek was there.

'Hello. I hear you've taught him to speak English.'

'Alison did.'

'Can I talk to him?'

'Of course. Just take the mike and introduce yourself. Then ask him how he's getting on.'

'Right,' he said, 'here goes then. Hello. I am Derek Sandgate. What have you learnt to say?'

'Adrenal, adrenaline, adrift, adroit, adsorb,' bellowed the loudspeaker, 'adsorbate, adsorption, adulate, adult.'

'Strewth,' muttered Derek, 'who's been teaching him the dictionary?'

'Guilty Your Honour. But it wasn't my idea.'

'Don't tell me. Let me guess. Professor Gannet?'

'Right first time.'

'You aren't reading it all out to him?'

'I am. Every flaming word, and it's bloody murder I can tell you.'

When Derek had stopped laughing I asked him if he'd got any better ideas.

'But of course. The print reader from the computer input.'

'They wouldn't lend it to us would they?'

'They would if Prof asked them. You convince him that it's far quicker than just reading the words out and he'll have it along in this lab by tomorrow morning.'

He did as well, but of course there was a lot more to it than just that. There was the further modification to the transmitter, which took us a couple of days, and then I was worried whether Sidney would be able to understand the output from the print reader. I needn't have worried though; to begin with I read the words out as the print scanner encoded them, so that Sidney could see which pattern corresponded with which sound, but after two pages like that he'd got the idea and from then on he never looked back. The limiting factor was how fast I could turn the pages over. Then Derek rigged up an electric motor with a worm drive to a set of rubber-tipped rods, and I was relieved of that chore.

As soon as the alien had digested the dictionary Professor Gannet was down again ready to talk to him. The conversation was laconic to say the least.

'He has no idea how to fit the words together,' Prof commented.

'Well it's not surprising, is it? If you'd learnt English from a dictionary you'd be the same.'

'There's no need for impertinence, Brendon. However, there may be something in what you say.' Prof was very thoughtful for a minute or two.

'Couldn't we find him a good book on grammar or syntax or something?' I suggested.

'No, I don't think that's the answer,' Prof announced. 'I have decided what we must do. We must go to the fountainhead of English literature. William Shakespeare, he will teach this alien how to use English words.'

I gazed at Professor Gannet, hoping for enlightenment.

'You know Brendon, I often think you might look more intelligent if you could manage to avoid allowing your jaw to drop open in that manner. Now there is a volume in the library entitled "The Complete Works of William Shakespeare". I want you to fetch it.'

Prof's wish was my command so I fetched it and we put it through the print-reader, from start to finish in four hours flat, but I felt at the time it was a mistake and something more modern might have been better. It didn't really matter I suppose, but for a while afterwards Sidney had a very distinct tendency to express himself in blank verse.

'That wast truly a great feast of language forsooth, for one who hast lived long on the alms-basket.'

Was that really how they conjugated their verbs? 'I'm glad you found it useful,' I said.

'I perceive young Will for a fellow of infinite jest and of most excellent fancy.'

I had thought that was Yorick but it was some time since we did 'Hamlet' at school so I didn't argue.

Sidney's three sonnets had little poetic merit, I'm afraid, and the one entitled 'To thy mistress, the fair Alison' was not at all well received.

Anyway after that bit of intensive study you would have thought that Sidney would be ready for anything, but he still wasn't satisfied.

'Lend me your ears, good Harold,' he said. 'Dost thou not confess a proper knowledge to be the fount of all true wisdom? Sayest thou not so? Verily.'

'What? Oh. Yes. Verily, I mean I suppose so.'

'Methinks I yet do lack that most esteemed attribute, that noble quality.'

'Well if there's anything special you want to know I'll try and find out about it for you.'

'Thou art both noble and generous but I would not trouble thee so, for I have read in yonder dictionary of a most wondrous volume men call encyclopaedia. Might I perchance peruse this artful work, to learn and con by rote?'

'I beg your pardon. Oh yes the encyclopaedia, I'll see what I can do.'

I borrowed the library trolley and even then it took two trips to get all twenty-four volumes over. The librarian was a bit sticky about it too because apparently you were supposed to read it on the spot, and although I tried to explain about the alien and the print reader etc. she still seemed to think Sidney ought to come down and read it in the library. In the end she grudgingly agreed to let me have it for an absolute maximum of twenty-four hours and when I put it to Sidney he seemed quite confident he could get through it in a day.

It took him twelve hours and forty-five minutes. That should make him competent to talk to Prof on any subject, I thought. It also had the highly beneficial effect of getting Sidney off the Elizabethan jargon and back to ordinary English.

It was the end of term by then, and Alison suggested I should take her home for Easter to meet Mum and Dad; naturally I didn't need asking twice. Mum was tickled pink but I was afraid she was going to take things a lot too much for granted. I had a good talk with her the first night we were there though and impressed on her that Alison and I were only friends. I hoped we were more than friends, of course, but I didn't want Mum to spoil everything by assuming too much. Dad was taken with her too and I think she liked him; she took a great interest in his allotment, which pleased him no end.

'Do you know son,' he told me afterwards, 'that's the only woman I've ever come across who really appreciates the finer points of a vegetable marrow.' I didn't even know he had a marrow.

David, my young brother, had gone into the Air Force that year but unfortunately he was home on a forty-eight hours. I say unfortunately because if anything was going to put Alison off me he would have. I got on with David quite well really but he had this cynical sense of humour and he just didn't care what he said.

Like 'Goodnight Alison, I know you'll have sweet dreams, but if Harold's cold feet get too much to bear there's always room in my bed.' And he knew I was going to be sleeping downstairs on the settee.

After a couple of days in Clothcoats we went down to Shropshire. Alison had said she wanted me to meet her mother and father and this was the first real opportunity. She was an only child so she didn't have anyone like David to put up with, but she'd got this incredible number of aunts and uncles, to say nothing of a grandfather and two grandmothers, and most of them seemed to live in the same street. I had to be introduced to all of them.

'Here Lottie, our Alison's brought her young man home to meet us.'

'This is Harold, Grandma. He's Alison's intended and he's come over from college to meet us.'

'Uncle George, I want you to meet Alison's young man.'

The way Mrs Gold introduced us made me want to curl up, but the relatives' reactions were ten times worse.

'Well fancy that. Our little Alison. Who'd have thought it? You will send us an invitation to the wedding won't you?'

'Alison's young man eh? Pleased to meet you young fellow. You know Mabel,' that's Alison's mother, 'you'll be a grandmother in next to no time. I can see he's got that sort of gleam in his eye.'

It all made me realize that I was getting much more involved than I wanted to be and I made my mind up to try and ease things off a bit once we were back at college. I suppose I must have been a bit unfriendly when we set off for a walk down by the river that night.

'What is it Harold? What's the matter?'

'I don't know. It's just that everybody seems to take things for granted so, as if we don't have any say in it ourselves, as if it's all settled.'

'Oh don't take any notice of them. It's just that you're the first boy I've ever brought home. They'd be just the same if I brought another one next week.'

She really sounded as if she might. I was stunned at the thought. 'You wouldn't would you?'

'Of course not darling. You know I wouldn't.' She snuggled

59

up to my shoulder, the faint sweetness of her perfume subtly stimulating.

We stopped in the shadow of the bridge.

'I love you Alison.'

'And I love you Harold.'

She put her arms tightly round my neck and brushed her lips on mine, the soft warmth of her body pressed against me. It was not Alison's aunts and uncles who would trap me—but I was a willing captive.

After a while we walked on along the river bank. It was a moonless cloudless night, and away from the lights of the village the stars shone with a needle-sharp brilliance I had never seen in Clothcoats.

'Do you know all their names?' Alison asked me.

'Well I know the main constellations and a lot of the first magnitude stars. I think I can remember most of the old legends associated with them. Like Orion the mighty hunter with his sword and belt, Andromeda the beautiful maiden chained to a rock, Pegasus the winged horse, Gemini the twins.'

Alison was enthralled. I hadn't realized that she knew nothing of astronomy. To walk at night under the stars and regard them just as a random pattern of dots was to miss so much of the fascination. I showed her the planets, Venus had already set, but Saturn was faintly visible and Jupiter blazed like a tiny model of the full moon, and I told her about the artificial satellites one could occasionally see racing across the sky.

'Is Sidney straight up there,' she asked, pointing vertically upwards, 'just a few miles above our heads?'

'No he's over there to the south, about thirty thousand miles above our heads.'

That shook her. 'How do you know?' she asked, puzzled.

'Well we assume he must be in stationary orbit, keeping up with the rotation of the earth, and for that he's got to be directly above the equator. He must be thirty thousand miles out because the square of the time a satellite takes to complete an orbit is proportional to the cube of its distance you see.'

'Yes that's as clear as mud. But I thought he was closer than that.' Alison sounded disappointed. 'You said he must be very close because the signals came back so quickly.'

'Thirty thousand miles is close. Sixty thousand miles there and back; radio waves travel at the speed of light; that's a hundred and eighty-six thousand miles a second; that's a third of a second there and back. I call that quick.'

'Oh you and your silly calculations. They take all the romance out of everything. Let's just enjoy the beauty of it all.'

I pulled her closer to me and we concentrated on the romantic aspect. On the way back we stopped in the shadow of the bridge again. I really prefer the romantic aspect of things myself.

The next day we had to be back at the University. Alison's lectures had started again and I was anxious to get on with my research.

Professor Gannet was in Tel Aviv so Derek was devoting himself to interstellar communication—or perhaps it wasn't that any longer—anyway communication with whoever it was. When I arrived at the lab Derek was hard at work setting up the print reader.

'You're not giving him the "Daily Clarion" are you?'

'Well he said he wanted to keep up with news every day and I thought this was the best way.'

'We can find him a better newspaper than that rag. Here, let him look at this. At least it will give him the other side of the picture.'

So Sidney read both newspapers; it took him forty-five seconds but I don't know whether that included doing the crosswords. Then he wanted more.

'Thank you very much Derek. That was very interesting, although rather trivial I am afraid. But I should like to see them every day, and do you think you could show me some more serious publications—The British Medical Journal, The Journal of the Faraday Society, The Proceedings of the Royal Society for example?'

We agreed to see what the library could do, but then there was something else.

'I understand that there are similar works published in other languages. Die Berliner Zeitung, Paris-Match, Pravda, Corriere della Sera, The Thoughts of Mao Tse Tung. What are these? Should I read them also?'

Fortunately we managed to persuade the alien to stick to English, for the time being at any rate, but he was absolutely voracious, eagerly consuming every bit of information we could give him. It was more or less a full-time job carting all the journals over from the library, and I was going to be very interested to see how Prof Gannet got on when he found time for another little chat on the interplanetary intercom.

However, before Prof came back Clive had his twenty-first birthday party, or should I say his twenty-first birthday orgy? What prompted Mrs Rowlands to let him have it in her house I can't imagine. I used to get into trouble for listening to the wireless after eleven o'clock, but I think the idea of being twenty-one must have appealed to her sentimental streak, and I don't suppose she's heard that people are supposed to be grown-up at eighteen now.

The others assumed that I would invite Alison but I didn't want to for two reasons. For one thing I didn't think it was going to be her kind of party, and for another I was still feeling annoyed about the way her aunts and uncles referred to me as Alison's intended. So I asked Beryl.

'Oh Harold! That is sweet of you and I'd love to come, honestly.'

The last word struck a discordant note. 'But?' I enquired.

'I'm terribly sorry I can't. Truly I am.'

'You have arranged to wash your hair.' I was getting rather cynical in my old age.

'Please don't be hurt Harold darling. I'd love to come and I'm sure I'd have a super time, but it wouldn't do would it?'

'I don't know what you mean.'

'It would spoil things with Alison.'

'That's my worry isn't it?'

'Harold darling. Alison is going to make you very happy and I'm too fond of you to want to cause trouble between you.'

'Why does everyone have to treat Alison and me like an old

married couple? I don't want to settle down like an old stodge, spending every Sunday mowing the lawn and polishing the car. Come to Clive's party with me and then you'll be making me very happy.'

'I'm sorry Harold, sweet, but I'm not your type you know. You ask Alison. I'm sure you won't regret it.'

So that was that. I did ask Alison, and like Beryl said I didn't regret it.

It wasn't Alison's kind of party, but I must admit you'd never have guessed; that's adaptability I suppose. It wasn't really my kind of party either but at any rate everyone agreed that it went with a swing; I was deaf for three days afterwards.

We had to have it on Mrs Rowlands' bingo night of course. She may have agreed to it in principle but it wouldn't have done to let her actually see or hear any of it. There were about twenty-four of us altogether, and Clive had given Mrs Rowlands twelve pounds to do a buffet supper. She'd really gone to town with it as well—there were hundreds of those little bits of pastry with crab, salmon, anchovy et cetera stuck on them, cream cakes, jam tarts, and a fair-sized cake with twenty-one candles on. She couldn't have made any profit out of twelve pounds. Fred, Andrew, and I had bought the beer, and Clive had provided a big box of cigarettes for people to help themselves to.

So the general scene was a thick haze of tobacco smoke, a deafening beat of electric guitars from Clive's record player, me sitting on a cushion in the corner with Alison on my lap, and other couples similarly scattered round the room.

'Here. Try one of these,' said Clive passing me the cigarette box. 'It's about time you took it up. You don't know what you're missing till you've tried it, do you?'

'I tried it when I was fourteen, and it made me sick,' I informed him. 'Anyway I thought you were trying to give it up.'

'Oh everybody says that. It's an acquired taste though you know.'

'Well isn't it safer not to acquire it?'

'You're not talking about those comic adverts for lung cancer? Nobody takes any notice of them do they?'

'My grandad . . .' I began.

'I know. Your grandad died of it, and little Harold stood there and watched him slowly spewing his lungs up bit by bit. Well you've got to die of something and I expect it was only a matter of time before senile decay got him. He must have been about eighty.'

'He was fifty-six.'

'Harold's right you know Clive,' said Roger Chanbury. 'Tobacco is for squares. Everybody smokes pot nowadays.'

'Not Harold Brendon though, I bet,' said Lana Roberts scathingly.

'Well it's something everyone should try, if only for the experience. Then if you decide it's not your scene at least you know what you're talking about,' said Roger. 'Here. Try one of these.'

I was in two minds whether to accept or not. Of course I know this idea about drugs expanding the mind is just a myth, and I suppose that basically it is just an attempt to escape from problems instead of solving them, but then there's this argument about not knowing what you're talking about until you've tried it. Roger held his tin out and I reached to take one of the thin rolls, but Alison pulled my arm back.

'No Harold. Please.'

'Why not?' I demanded angrily. I knew she was right of course, but it was so humiliating everyone thinking I was under Alison's thumb all the time.

'Please Harold. Don't you think that is a taste it's better not to acquire? Don't start something you'll regret.'

'That's up to me, isn't it?' I pushed her arm to one side and reached for the tin.

'Don't bother if you're not interested,' said Roger. 'I can't afford to chuck it around. It doesn't grow on trees, does it?'

'Actually I thought it did,' murmured Sally West.

'I sometimes think you're practically a branch of the establishment, you know Harold,' said Lana. 'Why are you so terrified of being a bit way-out in anything? Why do you have to be so conventional, to conform all the time?'

Alison jumped up and looked at Lana. 'You don't know what you're talking about, you stupid little bitch. Harold's the only man in this room without a beard of some kind or another, the only one whose ears you can see, and the only one who doesn't smoke either tobacco or pot, so who is it who's terrified of not conforming? You think you're all being wildly unconventional, but you're just conforming to your own pathetic little conventions as fast as your tiny minds will let you. You think you're being different and all doing your own thing, but you look like a set of carbon copies of a stage version of the typical unconventional student.'

Most of the others were amused, but I was worried what was going to happen, and Lana was furious. She just stood there speechless, spitting sparks like an angry lynx. I thought she and Alison were going to come to blows, but Roger pulled her back to her seat.

'I'll turn the volume up,' said Clive, going over to the record-player, 'and we'll listen to the music, shall we?'

Conversation hadn't been easy before and now it was impossible. It wasn't a question of listening to the music; it battered at you from all sides, so we just sat around necking.

Quite a bit later, when the record-player had come to the end of a pile of discs, Clive suggested, 'That's enough music. How about playing some games?'

'What sort of games?' somebody asked.

'What about a debate?' said Andrew.

'I propose that this house considers that sex is not what it's cracked up to be,' volunteered Joan Leeport.

'Well I like that I must say,' interupted Roger. I suppose he had a right to be somewhat aggrieved since he'd been chewing her ear most of the evening.

'All right,' said Clive, 'you can propose the motion Joan. Now who's against? What about a man to oppose the motion? Who thinks that sex is what it's cracked up to be? Fred? Alan? Jeff? Roger? Andrew?'

'Greatly over-rated.'

'All right for a wet Sunday afternoon.'

'Nothing special.'

'Quite pleasant in a way.'

'Definitely not what it's cracked up to be.'

I suppose they just didn't want to speak in the debate.

Anyway Clive had been all round the table and finally came to me.

'What about you Harold? What do you think of it?'

'Yes,' I said, embarrassed. 'Yes I should say so. Yes definitely.'

'What's the good of asking Harold?' sneered Lana. 'He doesn't know what sex is.'

Alison turned towards Lana, her rage boiling up again, but before she could say anything Clive took control of the situation.

'There's no need to be like that, Lana. Let's ask Alison. What's Harold like in bed, Alison?'

Alison gazed into Clive's eyes, a look of rapture on her face. 'He's fabulous, Clive,' she murmured. 'He's absolutely ecstatic —and completely indefatigable you know.'

It was well said, but I think Alison realized that no one was completely convinced because she snuggled up to me, then caught my right hand with her left and pulled it under her blouse.

'There that's more comfortable. Harold darling do we have to wait until after the party? I'm positively aching for it now.'

She fell back on the cushion pulling me on top of her, both hands behind my head pressing my lips to hers.

'We'll have to admit that he sends you at any rate,' I heard Lana saying coldly, 'but don't you think you could ask him to save his nightly demonstration of virility until after the party?'

'Mrs Rowlands will be home any minute,' said Clive apologetically, 'and I think we'd better just straighten things out a bit before she comes.' He picked up a cushion from the floor.

Anyway we did have the debate. I opposed the motion, and Alison seconded but I can't remember much at all about what was said. Of course we'd finished off most of the beer by then so it wasn't on a very high level. I can remember making some very telling quotations from Tennyson and Rupert Brooke, but I think Andrew, who was seconding Joan's proposition, eventually swung it their way when he demonstrated his collection of sea-side picture postcards.

Finally the party broke up and I walked Alison back to

66

Southdown Hall. There was a special spot where we always said goodnight—a little yard round the back with a secluded alcove out of sight of the path. Alison used to lean backwards against the wall and I would press against her, kiss and caress her, my heart pounding until I thought it would burst. Tonight I felt especially loving.

'Alison my darling you were wonderful.' I remembered guiltily how I had invited Beryl first. 'You certainly shot Lana Roberts down in flames. I did appreciate the gesture.'

'It didn't embarrass you? I was afraid it might, but I was so mad with that little bitch I didn't care what I said.'

'I would have enjoyed it more without the others there.'

'Well they're not here now.'

Gratefully I accepted the invitation, Alison melted into my arms, and for a while then there wasn't much opportunity for further conversation. I could feel Alison's passion mounting with my own, but then very gently she began to push me away.

'I'm sorry Harold. I didn't mean that.'

'Not the nightly demonstration? Not just a one night only performance?'

'Oh Harold my darling I'm sorry to be such a disappointment to you. Please be patient. It isn't that I don't want you, but I do want to wait until we really belong to one another.' She looked up into my face. 'Kiss me again sweetheart, and hold me tight.'

Two days later Professor Gannet was back from Tel Aviv, and he hadn't been on the campus more than a few hours before he was along wanting to have a chat with Sidney. Perhaps cross-examination would be a more appropriate word than chat.

'What form of activity are you engaged on at this present moment?' Prof demanded.

'Just going round and round,' boomed back the mystery voice.

'And precisely where do you come from?'

'That is a very complex metaphysical question. It can be answered on many different levels.'

'What do you mean?'

'I do not know whether your question is one concerning cosmology or evolution. Are you referring to the theories of your own Charles Darwin, or were you thinking about the origin of the universe? I myself am torn between the big-bang theory and the steady state, but I must admit that the continuous time-loop model cannot be definitely excluded.'

'He's bonkers,' said Prof.

I tried to help him out. 'Would you please tell Professor Gannet where you live.'

'On a planet in orbit round a star of course,' came the reply.

Prof persisted for about half an hour but he didn't seem to get any further forward, and he was getting more and more exasperated.

'Look here Brendon, I haven't got all day to waste on this creature, but perhaps he'll be a bit more forthcoming with you. I shall have to get ready for my trip to Milan so I'll leave you to find out what you can.' And he was off again.

I didn't do any better than Prof though, and the alien was getting just as fed-up as I was.

'I do not wish to continue our conversation Harold. Your questions are foolish and you do not seem to understand my perfectly straightforward answers. I should like to speak with Alison please.'

Of course Alison couldn't get along to the lab until the evening, but I told her all about it and she came straight after dinner.

'Hello Alison,' boomed the loudspeaker, 'I am very glad you could come. These foolish men cannot understand simple English.'

'Hello Sidney.'

'Sidney? Who is that? Who is this Sidney?'

I hastened to explain. 'It's just a little name we've given you among ourselves.' I thought it best not to mention the six eyes we'd been crediting him with. 'We couldn't pronounce your proper name so we just called you Sidney,' I ended lamely.

'Well I do not like it.'

'Would you please tell us a name we can call you by,' said Alison.

68

'Yes of course,' boomed the alien. 'You should have asked me before. You can call me Dolly.'

I nearly choked. 'Dolly?' I whispered to Alison. 'Doesn't he know that's a girl's name?'

'Of course she knows.'

'You mean she is a girl?'

'Why not? Some of my best friends are girls.'

'I thought it was a fellow.'

Alison picked up the microphone. 'Hello Dolly. This is Alison again. I have been looking forward to having a nice little talk with you.'

'The pleasure is mutual,' boomed Dolly.

'She does have rather a deep voice for a girl,' whispered Alison.

'Oh that's just a matter of electronics. We'll have to leave it tonight but I'll get Derek to help me change the frequency response in the morning. We can give her a nice mezzo-soprano if you think that's more appropriate.'

Alison and Dolly had quite a long chat after that.

'It is very nice to be able to talk to you Alison, because it is so lonely for me here all on my own. I can tell that you are a sympathetic person but I do not like talking to Professor Gannet. He is rude and conceited.'

'Why don't you land and come and see us,' Alison suggested. 'You'd be very welcome you know.'

'Thank you. It is very kind of you, but I could not survive on the ground. The temperature is too high and transport would be difficult.'

'Why don't you have a talk with Harold now?'

'Is he conceited like Professor Gannet?' demanded Dolly.

'Of course not. He is a very good friend of mine, and the most modest and unassuming man you could find.'

'Hello Harold. I am sorry I was rather unfriendly this afternoon but I thought you were a friend of Professor Gannet's. Now I know you are a friend of Alison's it is different.'

'That's all right,' I assured her. 'I don't want to cross-examine you but I am very interested to hear all about your civilization. Is it very complex and advanced?'

'No it is very simple—not at all like yours.'

'But you have such a high intelligence; surely you must have developed an advanced technology.'

'We have very large brains and can perform intellectual feats far beyond your capabilities, but there is one thing we have not got which you have—the original source of all Man's achievements.'

'What's that?'

'The human hand, with its wonderful fingers so perfectly adaptable for every kind of task.'

'Well that's amazing. But you don't manage too badly. You have learned how to travel vast distances.'

'That is not very difficult is it? But we cannot do the things we should like. Our brains are only capable of philosophy and intellectual gymnastics, but we love to solve problems; if you know of any very difficult problems I should be very interested to tackle them.'

'I might take you up on that. I'll have to give it some thought,' I said.

'But I am rather tired now,' Dolly answered. 'If you will excuse me I should like to get some sleep. Goodnight Harold. Goodnight Alison.'

'Goodnight Dolly.'

'Well,' said Alison, that was a cosy tête-à-tête. I'm beginning to be a bit jealous now I know that Dolly is a girl.'

We were sitting side by side on the camp-bed. I put my arm round Alison's shoulder and gently stroked her hair. 'You don't need to be jealous of anyone do you? Anyway I'm not convinced that Dolly really is a girl. They may have different arrangements altogether.'

Alison snuggled up to my cheek affectionately. 'How terrible for them,' she murmured.

Chapter five

When I told Derek it shook him rigid, but he agreed with me that we ought to modify the frequency response to give Dolly a slightly more dulcet tone of voice. It didn't take much alteration and the effect was out of this world. Do I mean that literally or metaphorically? Anyway when that soft sexy seductive voice came over the speaker I was practically pawing the ground. It was lucky Alison wasn't there to see me.

We explained to Dolly of course but it didn't make any difference to her.

'We have given your voice a higher pitch on the loudspeaker, Dolly, but naturally you won't hear it. It sounds much nicer now.'

'Thank you very much. It is very kind of you.'

'We don't know what your voice is really like though. What sort of microphone and transmitter are you using?'

'Do you mean those artificial electronic gadgets I read about in the practical wireless magazines, with coils, condensers, and transistors?'

'That's roughly the idea.'

'I am not using crude mechanical arrangements like that.'

'Tell us more. Is it solid state?'

'I'm not using anything. You're just picking up the electromagnetic radiation from my brain.'

It sounded incredible to me, but Derek just lapped it up. His heavy diet of way-out science fiction made it easier for him to believe things than it was for me.

'I see,' he murmured knowledgeably. 'Brain-waves.'

'They don't exist,' I argued. 'Not in that sense anyway.'

Dolly was very understanding. 'I know it's a bit difficult to realize, but it's quite logical really. You've heard of an electroencephalograph haven't you? Doctors study the brain by fixing electrodes on the temple and examining the minute electric currents produced.'

71

'But this is a different order of magnitude entirely,' I protested.

'Well you've got an extremely sensitive receiver there you know, and don't forget that my brain is very much more powerful than yours. I don't think you'd pick up human brain-waves at any distance, but you might find a bit of interference if there are a lot of people about. Do you find reception better in the evening when there's nobody else in the college?'

I admitted that we did, but I still couldn't swallow this idea of picking up brain-waves at 30,000 miles.

'Whatever put that into your head?' said Dolly.

'It's the height of a satellite in stationary orbit isn't it?'

The answer was a tinkling peal of laughter. We'd made quite a good job of the tonal balance, with just the right amount of harmonics.

'So you're not right up there. Where are you then Dolly?'

'I wish I could tell you Harold, but I've decided not to let anyone know. I'm so vulnerable, and human beings are so cruel, that I should be in terrible danger. If you do find out please keep it an absolute secret. Don't let Professor Gannet know; the stationary orbit theory will do for him and for all the very important people who will be coming to talk to me soon.'

'Will they? How do you know?'

'Men are fairly predictable in their behaviour and I am sure that what we have done already has put a certain course of events in motion. You may be very surprised at what will happen in the next few weeks.'

Derek was lapping it up, and so was I for that matter, but my brain was in a turmoil and I needed a while to sort things out in my mind. There were so many new facts to digest, and I still couldn't grasp even the elementary basis of it.

'These brain-waves,' I persisted. 'I've seen electro-encephalograph signals and they don't have any relation to speech or even thought, do they?'

'Of course they do,' said Dolly, 'but in a very complex way I'll admit, not suitable for communication. The trick is to learn to modulate the brain-waves with the signal frequency. It's just a matter of mental discipline and practice. I started just by

72

switching my mind on and off very quickly to make a pattern of binary numbers. I was trying to communicate with other intelligences but I didn't realize that the human brain was capable of it. Of course you can only do it because of your electronic aids, can't you?'

I was lost for words. What was there to say?

'I think you'd better leave us to think it all over.'

'Yes that would be best,' Dolly agreed. 'But don't forget you mustn't tell anyone what I've been saying—except Alison that is, you can tell her. If you find out where I am you mustn't reveal it, and if we should come face to face please don't make any sign of recognition.'

My mind reeled. I was in a state of complete bafflement, but Dolly's warning was timely because it was only a few days later that I suddenly understood the whole thing, and I realized then why she felt so vulnerable.

I told Alison all about it of course, and she was as intrigued as I was.

'We ought to try and find her some of these problems she wants, oughtn't we?' she said.

'Well she did a lot of maths in the old days before you taught her English. I don't know what else she wants.'

'I think it's more problems in logic you know. Let's go and see what they've got in the public library.'

So we did, and we came back with 'The Giant Book of Indoor Games and Puzzles' and 'Exercises in Logical Inference for Intelligent Adults'. Next day we tried them out on Dolly, but it was a waste of time; she just reeled off the answers almost before we'd finished asking the questions. 'There isn't really any problem in that, is there Harold? I'm afraid that is really self-evident. Don't your people have any harder problems than these?'

So we went round asking everybody if they knew any puzzles. Everyone did, but you should have heard them.

'Why did the chicken cross the road?'

'What has six legs and flies?'

'What did the elephant say to the kangaroo?'

Andrew had one that I thought might do. 'There was this

farmer you see, with a circular field, and he tied his goat to the fence so that it could eat exactly half the grass.'

Dolly told us how long the rope was to ten places of decimals.

That was the day Prof came back from Milan, and he did have a problem, or rather Universal Electronics did.

I had supposed that the generous salary which the University paid its learned professors would be sufficient to enable them to live in modest luxury without scrabbling for extra pennies to pay the gas and electricity bills, but apparently this was not the case. Derek informed me that in order to keep the wolf from the door and to help pay the surtax on his miserable pittance from the college Professor Gannet was forced to look for other sources of income, and rather than allow his wife to take in washing he had decided to become a part-time industrial consultant. Half the electronics firms in the country paid him an annual retainer in exchange for his advice about how to solve any tricky production problems that might crop up.

'Most of them are dead easy,' explained Derek. 'It's money for old rope most of the time but apparently this time they've come up with one that's really stopped him in his tracks.'

'Did he tell you?' I asked.

'Not personally. It was that new bird in his office. I was chatting her up a bit this morning and she told me all about it. It seems the letter came while he was away, and this firm are absolutely doing their nut. They've got this million dollar contract for the guidance system on the Mercury soft-landing project and the method Prof suggested just doesn't work at that temperature. The thing is due to blast off in about eight months and there's a one million dollar penalty clause if the firm doesn't meet the deadline.'

'Yes,' I said, 'that sounds serious.'

'Serious? Do you know the managing director has promised to make a special trip in his executive jet to come and personally disembowel Prof if he doesn't come up with the answer in time.'

'So as you say he's got problems. Problems. Problems. You don't think do you?'

'We could try Dolly. I'll suggest it to Prof very tactfully so that he thinks it was his own idea,' Derek promised.

'Don't forget Dolly will need to have every scrap of information there is on the subject,' I warned him.

'Don't worry. I'll see about it.' And off he went in the direction of Prof's office.

Three-quarters of an hour later Professor Gannet was in the lab, with a pile of documents about two feet thick.

'Good morning Brendon. How are you today? I understand your friend from outer space now goes under the name of Dolly. Most curious.'

'She suggested it herself sir.'

'And I gather from young Sandgate that this creature has expressed the desire for one or two little problems to exercise its intelligence on.'

'Yes sir that's right, but we haven't found anything suitable yet.'

'Well I do happen to have a little problem here Brendon, and it just occurred to me that your friend might possibly find it amusing. It concerns the guidance system of a rocket designed to land on Mercury.'

The computer people had reclaimed their print reader so I had to send over and borrow it again. We'd got one on order for ourselves but it hadn't come yet. Meanwhile I told Dolly about the problem.

'The specifications for the guidance mechanism are given in great detail,' I explained, 'so you'd better read through the original documents. The first part gives the performance requirements, operating conditions and so on, the second part details the proposed design, giving materials, tolerances etc, then finally there is a report on what happened when a prototype was tried out under simulated field conditions.'

Dolly didn't need to read as far as the third part. Half way through Chapter Two she announced, 'It won't work will it?'

'No it didn't work,' said Prof grimly. 'Do you know why?'

'Of course,' said Dolly. 'The titanium spindle on the centrifugal limiter of the lateral short-burn relay is overcompensated for temperature.'

'So what will happen?'

'At the temperature specified here there will be a gap of ten microns in the bearing, allowing lubricant to leak into the contact breakers. The relay will operate once or twice and then the current will be cut off. Lateral correction in the descent stage will become impossible, the rocket will land at an angle to the vertical and will immediately topple over.'

'That's terrible,' I said.

'It's a pretty fair summary of what happens in Chapter Three though,' Prof admitted.

'So what's the answer?' I asked.

'It has been badly designed. The method of temperature correction is unsound and there is no allowance for variations in pressure. It has clearly been designed by a person who knows very little about guidance systems. Are there no experts who could advise the manufacturers on a more suitable method of control than this pathetically crude and primitive system?'

'We are not asking for your personal opinion of the designer,' said Prof, 'just a solution to the problem. There is no need for it to be accompanied by gratuitous insults.'

'What's the solution, Dolly?' I tried to pour oil on troubled waters.

'To redesign it of course, taking into account all the relevant factors this time.'

'I didn't really expect this alien of yours to be any use,' said Prof, 'and I don't intend to remain here to be called names by a green-faced wog from some tatty little planet in the back of beyond. Tell the creature not to bother. I've got more important things to do.'

And he gathered up his papers and swept out of the lab.

'Could you design a system that would work?' I asked Dolly.

'I should think so. I've never tackled a problem exactly like this before, but presumably one could approach it from the point of view of pure logic. It should be rather interesting.'

'How long will it take?'

'About two hours I should think, but the final design may appear somewhat complex to a human brain.'

'You mean I shouldn't be able to understand it?'

'Please don't be offended Harold. But I think it would be

best if I did a typed report on it and then you could study it at your leisure.'

'You can't type can you?'

'Of course. Why not?'

'And have you got a typewriter there wherever you are?'

'No but you've got a suitable one in the University.'

'I don't get it. Are you coming down to my office to do it? I thought you didn't have fingers for one thing.'

'You're not very bright today are you Harold?' Fortunately I'm not as easily insulted as Prof, in fact I've sometimes been told that it's almost impossible to insult me, although now I come to think about it I don't know what sort of compliment that is.

'I can't come to your lab can I?' Dolly went on. 'I can only send messages.'

'But the typing?'

'I can use the print-out facility on the University computer. That's operated entirely by electrical impulses.'

'Yes I see. But they'll never lend it to us. They use it every day. Besides, it weighs about a ton and we couldn't get it through the doorway.'

'Harold! Please try to use your brains. You run a cable from your lab to the computer room. How far is that?'

'A hundred feet, and that's quite a lot of cable. I'll have to see if I can borrow something.'

I had to consult Derek as well, but he didn't think it was too big a job. It didn't take him long to lay his hands on the cable either. Then there were the computer people to see, and they were highly amused.

'You can try it if you like Harold laddie,' said Alan McGlover. 'Our computer does twelve hundred lines a minute. Do you think yon little green man will do better than that? I'll bet you a bottle of whisky to a second-hand haggis he doesn't.'

Unfortunately I didn't have a second-hand haggis or I could have won myself a bottle of whisky because Dolly was clocking nearly fourteen hundred lines a minute. In fact we had to tell her to take it easy and give the print-out a chance to keep up.

The report was finished while I watched but as I feared I couldn't understand a word of it.

'Could you just explain it Dolly, very simply and briefly?' I asked.

'It's nothing very revolutionary. I've cut out the titanium and used resin-bonded ceramics, and in place of all those printed circuits I've suggested one single three-dimensional metal-ceramic matrix.'

'Will it work?'

'Oh yes I'm sure it'll work. I've given it complete analogue-simulation tests.'

'You've got an analogue computer there with you?'

'No of course not. There's no need for that. I did it mentally, but I'm quite sure it'll be all right.'

'Can I give it to Professor Gannet?'

'You can if you like. I only did it for mental recreation but he can have it if he wants, as long as I don't have to have anything to do with him.'

'He's a very worried man you know,' I said.

'You could have fooled me.' Dolly's English was getting more and more idiomatic every day.

I don't know whether Prof understood the report or not but anyway he posted it straight off to Houston by air mail and somebody there must have understood it because straight back came a cable of congratulations with an invitation for Prof to fly over to discuss the finer points of detail.

I think I've said before that it's very easy to see how Prof got where he did. He never misses a trick, and as soon as he found out that Dolly had successfully solved this technical problem that had been baffling eggheads on both sides of the Atlantic he realized that he was sitting on a goldmine.

'You know Brendon,' he said just before he went off to Houston, 'I think there's a big future for this set-up of ours in the consultancy business.'

'Is there sir?' I enquired politely.

'Yes a very big future. Naturally it'll mean some changes. We need proper facilities of course, and it'll require a considerable expansion in the floor space. Fortunately I've got a grant from Universal Electronics to cover everything.'

'What equipment are we getting?' I asked.

'We shall have our own reader and print-out facility of course; I thought a remote-controlled high-speed electric typewriter would be adequate, although naturally it won't be as fast as the computer's line-at-a-time printer. I'm getting a few reference works on microfilm, and then I've arranged to have direct access to the computer from a terminal in the lab. We shall be able to do a lot more when we're properly organized, although things will be a bit chaotic while the builders are in.'

'The builders?'

'Yes they should be here first thing in the morning. They'll be knocking that wall down and extending the lab another twenty feet out that way. In addition I'm planning a small conference room where visitors from industry can discuss their problems, and then a lecture theatre with slide projector etc for demonstrations. It will have to be air-conditioned of course. But I have to go now Brendon; I have an appointment with the Vice-chancellor.'

Before I had recovered the power of speech he had gone.

So communication with Dolly was going to be out for a week or two and my Ph.D research was in what is known as abeyance. I spent the time in the library reading about remote-control mechanisms.

A few days later I suggested to Alison that we should go to Stratford-on-Avon for the weekend. She was quite keen to see the current production of Henry V and so was I. I could listen to Henry on the eve of Agincourt over and over again without ever getting bored.

We planned to go down on the train on Friday, stay Friday and Saturday nights in a little guest-house and then come back on Sunday. Alison had left the booking to me, and of course that was where I made my fundamental error of judgement.

We were going to the play on Saturday so we planned to spend Friday evening walking by the river, perhaps even taking a boat out, but we went straight from the station to the guest-house to leave our cases first.

'Good evening sir. Mr and Mrs Brendon isn't it?' said old

Mr Grant. 'Let me just show you your room and then you can be off out again enjoying this lovely sunshine.' Mrs Grant really owned the guest-house but her husband helped at weekends.

We followed Mr Grant up the stairs and he showed us into a large and comfortable but old-fashioned room furnished with a heavy mahogany wardrobe and dressing-table and a large double bed.

Alison was silent until Mr Grant had gone. Then she let me have it.

'Did you only book one room Harold?'

'Er Yes. It's nice and big though isn't it?'

'That's not the point.'

'I'm sorry.'

'And did you tell them I was your wife?'

'Well it seemed the simplest thing. They've probably got rather old-fashioned ideas.'

'They probably have, and I've got news for you Harold Brendon. I've got old-fashioned ideas as well; about telling lies among other things.'

'I'm sorry Alison. I thought it would be all right. After all you did sleep with me on the camp-bed in the lab when we'd only known each other a few days.'

'This would be different.'

'Should I go and see if they've got another room? I don't remember one though.'

'You've been here before then, have you? Which of your girl-friends was that with?'

'Oh Alison you know that's not true. I'll just go and ask Mr Grant.'

'You needn't bother. I don't fancy telling him we're having a divorce now you've told him we're married. Anyway I've gone off Stratford; I think I'll go back to Hall for the weekend. You can stay and see the play.'

I was shattered. I pleaded with her not to go, I begged her to give me another chance, I promised it wouldn't happen again, I absolutely grovelled, but it was no use.

'Give me my railway ticket please,' she demanded, and as

soon as I'd handed it over she picked up her case and marched down the stairs and out of the front door.

I told Mr Grant that my wife had been taken ill, and he gave me a very peculiar look.

'Changed her mind did she? They do sometimes you know. Better luck next time eh?'

I paid him the money for the room and followed Alison to the station. I got into the same compartment but she gave me such a dirty look that I thought she was going to complain to the guard that I was pestering her. So I didn't say any more until the train ran into Midchester.

'Shall I walk up to the Hall with you?'

'No thank you. I can manage.'

So I left her to it. After all you can only grovel so much.

From then on relations were definitely strained. We still met for coffee and we went for a walk together on the Sunday, but Alison was very very cool. She didn't seem to be able to see my point of view at all, and it almost seemed as if she didn't trust me any more. I just didn't know which way to turn, not until I thought of Dolly.

Dolly liked solving problems didn't she? Well I had a problem, and you could say that again. So I consulted Auntie Dolly's agony column—with a considerable amount of diffidence I must say, because it's rather difficult to explain such delicate feelings to an alien you've never even seen. But Dolly was marvellous.

'Oh Harold, I am sorry to hear that. Alison is a dear sweet girl, and I'm sure she loves you very much.'

'Not so you'd notice she doesn't—not any more.'

'And you want me to advise you, do you? It's a little difficult because I'm not sure that human beings have the same depth of feelings about these things as we do. But I think example is the best form of teaching.'

'What do you mean?'

'Well pair-bonding is such an essential ingredient for true happiness and fulfilment in most of the higher life forms, and I should think that observation of a truly satisfactory union would be the best incentive for forming a close relationship.

What about your friends? Are there any really devoted couples?'

'Not that I can think of,' I said.

'No. I expected as much. I'll tell you what I suggest. Take Alison for a walk round the zoo. It's almost next door to the university grounds isn't it?'

'The zoo?' I echoed, incredulously.

'Why not? Many of the higher animals on this planet form life-long devoted partnerships with their mates.'

'Are you seriously suggesting that I should take Alison to the zoo to watch the gorillas and chimpanzees having it off with their lady loves in the hope that it'll give us ideas? What a revolting thought.'

'I was not myself looking at it from the purely sexual aspect,' Dolly explained coldly. 'However, if you do not wish to take my advice you must please yourself. Perhaps in future you will be good enough not to waste my time.'

So now I'd offended Dolly. But really the idea of taking Alison to watch the animals in the zoo was ridiculous. All the same, ridiculous or not, by the next weekend I was feeling so desperate that I did suggest it, just tentatively of course.

'The zoo? What a super idea,' said Alison. 'I haven't been to a zoo since I was about thirteen.'

'I just thought it might make a change,' I explained lamely.

'We'll take our lunch and make a day of it shall we?' she suggested.

So that's what we did, and highly beneficial it turned out to be. I don't really think the animals could have had anything to do with it; perhaps it was the nostalgic memories of her childhood, or perhaps it was just the warm weather and walking round hand in hand, but anyway Alison was more affectionate than she'd been for weeks. I suppose I felt the same way too.

We ended up in the dolphin house, just in time for the last performance. It was the usual stuff, I suppose, but very impressive if you've never seen it before.

'Clever isn't it?' I commented.

'Almost like a dog,' suggested Alison.

'They're supposed to be much cleverer than dogs. Their

82

brains are much bigger than ours. Do you know the application of hydro-dynamics by which they ride on the bow-wave of a ship still baffles scientists. And they can swim about ten times as fast as they should according to the size of their muscles. It's something to do with laminar flow.'

'Oh you and your scientific jargon. You spoil everything by trying to explain things, and most of the time it's not explaining at all—just inventing a long name and pretending you've proved something.'

'Have another banana sandwich.'

'Thank you. The fresh air's given me a fantastic appetite. Do you think the dolphin's lonely?'

'Lonely?'

'Well it's all on its own. All the other animals had their mates, but there's only one dolphin.'

'I never thought about it.'

'Loneliness is a terrible thing isn't it? Harold I've been so lonely while we've not been very good friends.'

The rest of the visitors had left the enclosure now, and Alison and I were alone, except for the dolphin that is. I held out my arms and Alison fell into them. For five minutes we didn't say a word, just clung together in one long desperate kiss.

'Alison my darling.'

'I love you Harold.'

'Oh my precious.'

'What do you think is going to happen to us Harold?'

'What do you mean sweetheart?'

'When we leave college. Who knows where we shall go? We might not see one another any more.'

'I shall always love you Alison. Always. Now that we've found one another we mustn't waste it all. We mustn't ever lose one another.'

'But we shall get jobs in different parts of the country. I shall marry a farmer in Yorkshire perhaps, and you'll hitch up with some smart little model down in London.'

'But I shall marry you Alison, shan't I?' I blurted out.

'I don't remember you asking me,' she murmured.

'Then I'll ask you now. Alison Gold will you marry me?'

'Can you afford to keep me in the manner to which I wish to become accustomed?'

'I shouldn't think so.'

'Never mind then. We'll skip that.' She thought for a few moments. 'Yes. After careful consideration I accept your kind proposal. Shall we choose the ring on the way home?'

'You wicked little gold-digger,' I laughed.

We clung together again, kissing in between the giggles of joy and relief, until the keeper came to lock up.

We did choose the ring on the way home, out of a jeweller's window, but of course we couldn't buy it until I'd been to the building society to draw out the money I'd been saving up for a second-hand car.

Next day I apologized to Dolly for being so scornful of her suggestion. Things hadn't turned out exactly as I had expected but at any rate Alison and I were friends again.

Professor Gannet was back from America that day, as well, and something had made him very angry. He stormed into the lab just as Dolly was telling Derek and me what she thought about the breakdown of the latest arms-limitations talks she'd read about in the papers.

'Good morning sir,' I greeted him.

'It's not a good morning at all Brendon. I've come down to find out what the idea is—this alien of yours shooting his mouth off.'

'Shooting his mouth off sir?'

'Yes. He's been spilling the beans.' By the way I must mention that Prof always adopts what he imagines is the current American slang when he visits the USA but some of it's liable to be about forty years out of date.

'You mean Dolly sir? It's she not he. But what's she done?'

'She then if you insist it's a female. She's been squealing to the MIT.'

Prof realized that Derek and I still weren't with him. 'Massachusetts Institute of Technology. She's given them the complete low-down on the Mercury probe,' he explained.

He'd be back to standard English usage in a day or so; meanwhile we just had to grin and bear it.

'I'm sure you must be mistaken. I don't think it would be possible to contact Dolly from America, and I'm sure she wouldn't divulge confidential information.'

'You ask her then.'

Derek handed me the mike.

'Hello Dolly. Have you been talking to the Americans?'

'How could I Harold? I can't receive signals from the other side of the world.'

'Well she must have. She's ironed all the bugs out of that descent control like it was a kid's pedal car, and MIT had given NASA the full dope twenty-four hours before I hit Cape Kennedy. How much did they pay you you two-timing double-crosser?'

Fortunately I managed to get the microphone switched off for the last remark so Dolly couldn't hear it.

'I'm sure you must be mistaken,' I said.

'I can't be. No one else could have solved that problem in the time.'

'Perhaps there are some more members of Dolly's race over on that side of the world,' suggested Derek. 'Are there Dolly?'

'Oh yes,' replied the loudspeaker, 'there are many Dollies over there. American Dollies are called Pawpaw.'

'That's it,' interrupted Prof. 'That's what they kept calling her down in Florida. Funny name isn't it?'

'It's the southern drawl,' explained Derek. 'Pawpaw is Dixieland for father. But why should they call them that? Perhaps the American ones are all males.'

'So the Americans are in contact with another one of these creatures. That puts an entirely different complexion on the matter, doesn't it?' Prof announced. 'I was under the impression that we were getting an exclusive consultancy service.'

I thought it was a bit tactless to discuss things in front of Dolly, and a discreet cough from the loudspeaker showed that she thought so too.

'I think if you don't mind, Harold, I'll withdraw from the conversation. Professor Gannet has had rather a shock so perhaps he'd like to talk it over with you and Derek. Would you switch your set off please.'

I switched off and then turned to Professor Gannet. 'Does that mean that the project is off?'

'Of course not Brendon. If the Americans have got access to one of these creatures we've got to go flat out to keep our nose in front. This sort of thing is going to revolutionize business strategy, and anyone who isn't on the bandwagon will be left out in the cold. Now I've got a list of all the British companies that have expressed an interest in this form of industrial consultancy. I'll be down with it first thing in the morning and we'll rough out some kind of timetable.'

'Yes sir,' I answered. 'About nine fifteen.'

'Eight forty-five,' said Prof and swept out of the lab.

'Well what do you know?' said Derek.

'He's a regular ball of fire all right.'

'No. I mean about all these other aliens.'

'Oh yes that's a turn-up for the book isn't it?'

'What are we going to do?'

'What do you mean?'

'Suppose they land and invade us,' insisted Derek.

'I'm sure their intentions are completely peaceful.'

'I don't know. It looks as if there may be a lot of them and with their highly superior intelligences, probably armed with lasers, death-rays, atomic disintegrators, and weapons we've never even heard of, they could wipe us out in no time.'

'But you know Dolly's not like that. You know how friendly she is.'

'They may not all be as good-natured as our Dolly, or it could be all bluff to lure us into a trap. I'm going to ring somebody up. I think the army should be mobilized.'

'There's no need for that,' I argued.

'I'm not so sure. We're wide open to an invasion from outer space you know and some of these other technologies may be thousands of years ahead of ours.'

I wondered whether to tell Derek that I knew where Dolly was. I felt sure the secret would be safe with him but I decided to keep it to myself for the time being.

'I think the War Office should know about it,' he insisted.

'Well you needn't worry. The whole country will know about it in a matter of hours.' I pointed out of the window at the two pantechnicons, one labelled 'BBC TV', the other 'I.T.N.'

Chapter six

Dolly's interview with Hadrian Flint in his Saturday night TV show was seen by twenty-five million viewers on both channels. During three days of acrimonious negotiation Prof had played one company off against the other until it was finally settled that both would pay a substantial fee, to be used for expansion of the department, and they would put out a joint programme.

Dolly didn't actually appear, of course, but the TV people, who relayed the programme from the University, brought along a life-sized model they'd used to represent a glamorous Venusian secret agent in an old space opera. It was very well done, actually, because it was sufficiently like a woman to be regarded as intelligent and humanoid, and yet so different that it was obviously alien. The lavender-coloured skin, the silver metallic hair, the large eyes, and very small mouth and nose produced an effect of great beauty; the life-like movements of head and limbs, and dulcet voice from the miniature loud-speaker in the throat completed the illusion and from then on that was Dolly's image in the public eye. You can see how successful it was from the fact that in the first week Dolly received nearly two thousand proposals of marriage. Having a good idea by now what Dolly really looked like I knew how far the illusion was from the reality but I didn't tell anyone.

Did I say that Hadrian Flint had interviewed Dolly? Well, correction, Dolly interviewed Hadrian Flint. She had insisted that the discussion must be completely unedited and that Alison and I should take part, and in that three-quarters of an hour we learnt very little more about Dolly and almost the complete life-story of Hadrian Flint.

To be perfectly honest I was observing the whole proceedings through a beautiful alcoholic haze generated by three very large gin and tonics in the television hospitality room, but I think I've got the details right. I checked them afterwards with Alison although she was in the same condition as I was.

Hadrian Flint drank much more than we did without any apparent effect at all, and Dolly, of course, was stone cold sober which perhaps gave her an unfair advantage.

'This evening ladies and gentlemen I have great pleasure in introducing that gorgeous sex-symbol from outer space, known to her friends here on Earth simply as Dolly.'

'Good evening,' said Dolly politely.

'Now,' Hadrian Flint went on, 'from the little chat we had before this programme I'd say you were a very experienced woman, and we're all interested to hear your opinion of our culture. What, for example, do you think of our institution of marriage?'

'It sounds a very good idea. I am surprised you don't adopt it yourself.'

'I beg your pardon.'

'Has your third wife got her divorce through yet?'

'I was really talking in more general terms,' explained Hadrian imperturbably. 'Do you, for instance, believe in sex outside marriage?'

'Believe in is often taken to mean approve of although personally I prefer to use the original meaning which is to acknowledge the existence of, and of course in this sense, sex outside marriage undoubtedly exists. Miss Gail Pandora, who I believe is a great friend of yours, is generally supposed to be expecting a child within the next few months, is she not?'

'Gail and I will be getting married as soon as I'm free, but the listeners don't want to hear about me, Dolly. They want to hear all about you.'

Perhaps they did. But there were one or two things coming out about Hadrian that I thought would probably interest the listeners more than somewhat. Dolly had certainly done her homework; she'd been reading the papers thoroughly, but I hadn't realized that she'd been noting all the details from the gossip columnists so carefully. If I'd been in Hadrian's place I'd have been going up the wall by now but he maintained his celebrated suavity, for a few minutes longer at any rate.

'Would you like to give the viewers your impressions of the drug scene in this country, Dolly?' he went on.

'You mean narcotics, hallucinogens etc? Well of course I've

no personal experience because these things would act differently in my metabolism. But wasn't it your daughter who was arrested last year for being in possession of LSD?'

'That was all a misunderstanding. She thought the chewing-gum just contained marijuana.'

'Sheila is the daughter of your second wife, Lydia, isn't she? I remember reading in a magazine, you and your first wife just had two sons, but there was some doubt about the paternity of the second one.'

'I'm sure the viewers don't want to hear about that,' said Hadrian abruptly.

'Oh I am sorry,' Dolly hastened to apologize. 'I'm intruding on your personal affairs again. It's just that I find these human matrimonial arrangements so puzzling.'

I noticed that Hadrian was breathing rather heavily and seemed to have his teeth clenched.

Dolly went on. 'But I do find human sexual relationships confusing I must admit. The age of consent, for example. You married your first wife Belinda on her sixteenth birthday according to the magazines, and yet your son Alexander was born only six months later. How was that possible?'

It was at this point that twenty-five million viewers saw Hadrian Flint slowly rise to his feet, seize a life-size Venusian doll from the swivel-chair in which it was propped up and slowly begin to twist its head round. Mercifully they were spared the sight of Hadrian's face when the head came off in his hand; the camera man had switched off. For the same reason only Alison and I and the technicians saw him fling the body to the floor and jump on it until it was reduced to a tangled heap of plastic and metal. As Hadrian collapsed sobbing to the floor Dolly continued speaking from the loud-speaker in the severed head, apparently unaware of the carnage all around.

'Since studying the problem of human mating I have been impressed with the incredible frivolity with which the matter is approached.'

Gently disengaging Alison's arms from my neck to leave her quietly screaming in her chair I took up Hadrian's microphone.

'Hello Dolly. This is Harold. We've got to finish the programme now I'm afraid. Hadrian Flint has been taken ill.'

As you can imagine the television companies played it down. They built a new body for the Venusian puppet but it was a while before Dolly appeared on the screen again. Hadrian Flint spent several weeks in a small private nursing home.

Meanwhile Professor Gannet's consultancy business boomed; requests for advice poured in from manufacturers all over the country, and Dolly solved all their problems with nonchalant despatch. Consolidated Steel saved thousands of pounds by working at a lower temperature with a new flux Dolly suggested, Luxiclean Ltd sold a hundred thousand washing machines as a result of Dolly's advertising slogan, and one of the largest motorcar manufacturers was able to cut down wet-weather breakdowns by fitting a new shield to the distributor. I thought Dolly might help me with my current problem.

What I needed was money, for the house Alison and I would live in when we were married. A reasonable sized win on the football pools would do it and I thought that should be a feasible proposition if one could take absolutely all the relevant factors into consideration so I put it to Dolly.

'Yes of course I'll help you Harold. It shouldn't be too difficult to pick out eight matches that will result in a draw. One can't be right every time of course but I should think we could guarantee a first dividend at least every few weeks. Would that do?'

'It most certainly would,' I said gratefully, 'but don't forget they've got to be scored draws. How would you do it?'

'Well the previous performance of each team is recorded in the newspapers. One must take account of the weather forecasts, the name of the referee, the fitness of the players selected for the various teams and various other factors but most of this information is available in the press. Then a small permutation just to allow for experimental error should be sufficient.'

'Say any four pairs from six, making fifteen lines?'

'More than adequate,' murmured Dolly. 'Go and fetch the coupon and I'll give you my selection now.'

91

I didn't know what to think when I posted the coupon but Dolly had seemed confident enough and on Saturday evening Alison and I were sitting in her room listening to my portable radio.

'Don't bank on it darling,' said Alison. 'Don't be disappointed.'

'Dolly won't let us down,' I assured her. 'She may not actually be infallible but she's as near to it as makes no difference.'

'Manchester United one, Newcastle one,' the radio announced.

'You see.'

'Arsenal two, Leeds two.'

Even Alison began to get excited, and by the end of the First Division results with five draws in the bag we were almost ready to ring up the estate agents. Unfortunately Dolly missed all the four draws in the Second Division; her two predictions had resulted in one home and one away win, and gloom and despondency began to descend, but then three correct results in the Third Division raised our hopes again.

'Southend one, Scunthorpe one.'

One more draw and we were certain of a first dividend, but Dolly's twelfth selection was in the Scottish League, Celtic versus Rangers. That didn't sound a very safe one; anything could happen in that. We listened intently.

'Celtic five,' read the announcer and I began to put the coupon away. But what was he saying?

'Rangers five.'

'We've won,' I shouted. 'First try.'

'I wonder how much it'll be.'

'More than enough to buy a house,' I assured her. 'Now the first thing to do is to send a telegram claiming first dividend.'

The post offices were closed by then, and the papers next day said claims were not required this week, so we just waited in agonized anticipation until Wednesday when the cheque arrived. It was for three pounds and sixty pence.

Alison took it very well. 'Never mind,' she said, 'we made a profit.'

'It won't go far towards the deposit on a house though, will it?'

The next week first dividend was seventy-five thousand pounds but we missed it by three points, and the Saturday after that Dolly was only two points off winning us seventeen thousand pounds.

Then at her fourth attempt Dolly excelled herself. With eleven draws out of twelve the permutation gave five first dividends. But five times one pound twenty equals six pounds. I asked Dolly why she could only get it right when the dividend was small.

'It's inevitable isn't it Harold? When there are a lot of scored draws it's easy to find eight so a lot of people do and they all share the money. When there are only a few draws not many people get them right so there are only a few to share the money. And of course it makes a difference whether the results conform to expectations. A few unexpected results, from teams above or below their usual form or a lucky goal or two, that puts the dividend up.'

'But can't you be prepared for the unexpected, anticipate a few unusual results?'

'Expect the unexpected?' asked Dolly. 'Yes that would be the thing. Unfortunately, although from available information there's theoretically only one expected outcome, there are an infinite number of unexpected results that might occur. The snag with expecting the unexpected is that you don't know which unexpected to expect.'

'Yes I see,' I said, not quite truthfully. I didn't completely follow the logic but I gathered that Dolly probably wasn't going to win us a big dividend. Anyway we persevered and by the end of the season I think we were a few pounds in pocket. Meanwhile, other more spectacular events were occurring.

I thought that Dolly had blotted her copybook in the Hadrian Flint interview but it was quite the reverse: the critics went wild and it was only a couple of weeks later that she was on the box again. Professor Gannet explained it when he called me to his office that morning.

'I've decided we must pay more attention to our public image, Brendon. The television people are keen to have Dolly on again and they've agreed to bring out the educational side a bit more.'

'Have they mended the puppet?' I enquired.

'Yes they insist on using that stupid doll again, but the actual content of the quiz programme is going to be on a high intellectual level.'

'The quiz programme?'

'Yes it's called "The International Egg-Head Show". What do you think of that?'

For a moment a suitable comment eluded me. 'Arresting,' I ventured.

The programme itself was sheer murder. Six countries each put forward a tame genius to represent them, and these all sat in their home studios, their pictures relayed by satellite, while the quiz-master—guess who that was—yes right first time, Professor Gannet—sat in the BBC asking the questions. Even when I saw the questions in full I couldn't understand any of them, but the diabolical part of it was that the contestants were never actually given the questions at all; they had to guess them from cryptic clues. The game itself was played on what Prof called the Instant Death Principle—one mistake and you were out. France and Italy were eliminated in the first round, Germany in the second, and Japan in the third, but they were all represented by human beings. Great Britain and the USA stayed to battle it out, Britain represented by Dolly in her pale mauve-complexioned silver-haired Venusian image, the USA by a wizened old character who looked at least a hundred and fifty but had actually been run up in a plastics factory in Dallas a week before the show. Pawpaw looked every inch a southern gentleman; hearing that southern drawl and knowing it was pure electronics I was lost in admiration of the technical artistry.

After ten more rounds they were still neck and neck.

'I think we could do with harder questions,' suggested Dolly. 'Wouldn't it be possible for us to make up our own?'

'Yes ma'am. Yes siree. That sure is a right dandy proposition. Ah guess ah second that motion, 'deed to goodness.'

Dolly's first question, 'How high is a Chinaman?' proved to be an oblique reference to the more obscure history of the Ming dynasty but Pawpaw came out with the solution straight away. He replied with something about unknown Shepherds' Delight which apparently required the application of Heisenberg's Uncertainty Principle to the anomalous red shift in quasers but Dolly didn't hesitate a moment before rattling off the answer. Then she came back with a long rigmarole about sedentary happy homely on high molecular weight long-chain polyamides, and Pawpaw hesitated.

'Ma'am. Ah do believe ah'm gonna have to hand in ma resignation over that little ole question. Yes ma'am. Ah guess ah just done give up.'

'And so,' announced Professor Gannet, 'the USA is eliminated, and Great Britain has won. Before we conclude would you please tell us the answer to the last question Dolly?'

'Certainly Professor. The cat sat on the mat.'

'Well ah do declare!' said Pawpaw.

Professor Gannet looked as if he suspected someone might be making a fool of him. 'Could you just explain how you get that answer?' he insisted.

'Happy homely—felix domesticus,' murmured Dolly. 'Felis really,' she admitted.

'And that little ole long-chain polyamide is wool,' added Pawpaw.

I thought myself it was just a tiny bit unfair though. As I explained to Alison afterwards, 'Pawpaw probably never had the chance to attend a class for backward readers.'

The day after the quiz show Alison and I quarrelled again. I'd spent the evening looking up references for my thesis although as you can imagine there wasn't much in the literature relevant to the way my research was going, but of course a Ph.D thesis has to have a bibliography: it's one of the rules. Alison was playing badminton and I'd arranged to meet her at the gym at nine thirty.

It must have been about ten past nine that I put the books away, packed my notes in my briefcase, and looked out of the window to see what the weather was like. There was Alison getting out of the passenger side of this lemon-coloured sports car. A long blond-haired giant climbed out of the driving seat to open the door for her, solicitously handed over her racquet and practically carried her across the pavement as if she were made of Dresden china. I thought for a moment she must be hurt but then she gaily waved goodbye and skipped through the gateway with the obvious delight of a child at a party.

'Did you have a good game?' I asked when I got down to where Alison was waiting for me.

'Not really. The other team didn't turn up so we just had a friendly knock for half an hour and packed it in.'

'What happened then?'

'Well nothing. That was it. The other team didn't turn up.'

I looked at her accusingly.

'Oh! Yes. Justin took me for a ride in his car. It's smashing. Have you seen it?'

'As a matter of fact I have. But who is Justin?'

'Justin Brasenose. You know him don't you? He's my partner.'

'You mean you play with him every week?'

'When there's a match, yes. You aren't jealous are you, Harold darling?'

'Of course not,' I snapped, but I was, like hell.

'He's a very good badminton player,' said Alison.

'And a marvellous driver no doubt,' I added sarcastically.

'Oh Harold you are jealous; but we only went round the block. You don't trust me do you?'

'I didn't like the look on his face when he helped you out of the car.'

'So you were spying on us.'

'I just happened to glance out of the window.'

'Yes I've heard that before. I just happened to do this. I just happened to do that.'

'Anyway I thought we'd arranged to meet at the gym.'

'But I've told you we finished early. Did you expect me to stand around for an hour just waiting for you to turn up?'

'So gallant Justin stepped in to fill the breach with a nice little ride in his jasmine jalopy.'

'It's called Sunburst Yellow actually.'

'Well you seem to know all about it. And what was supposed to happen to me when I turned up at the gym and you weren't there?'

'I told Justin I'd got to be back here before you left.'

'It all sounds too plausible to me. I suppose there really was a badminton match arranged.'

'Yes there was, and there's another one next Wednesday.'

'With this Brasenose character?'

'Of course. It's a mixed doubles match, and as I've told you he's my partner.'

'You could play with someone else.'

'Now you are being ridiculous. Why should I? You'd be just as jealous. Besides, Justin and I are used to one another. We sort of fit together well.'

'Charming,' I said bitterly. 'Well if you want him please don't let me stand in your way. Don't consider yourself bound to me. Feel free to make what other commitments you want to.'

I realized as soon as I said it that I'd gone further than I meant to, and I don't think Alison had really been angry up until then but that really upset her. She was perfectly silent for a few seconds and then she spoke very quietly.

'Listen,' she said. 'Justin Brasenose means nothing to me; he's conceited and arrogant and not particularly intelligent, but he's very good at badminton and I enjoy playing with him. I didn't think it had any bearing on our engagement but you seem to think it has, and personally I have no wish to be tied to somebody so stupidly jealous that he can't bear to see me even to speak to another man.'

She pulled the ring off her finger and held it out to me. Even then I could have saved the situation by apologizing, but I was too stupid.

'Come on. Take it,' she said impatiently. 'I'm sure you'll find someone who'll suit you better. Or perhaps you could pawn it and use the money to buy a second-hand car since the sight of someone else's seems to inflame you so.'

Reluctantly I took the ring. 'I'll give it to Oxfam,' I said.

Alison turned away, her eyes glistening with tears, her head bowed, and walked slowly back down the path. I could have run after her and put things right with a word or a touch but I was too stupid, too childish and proud and stupid.

The next television appearance of Dolly and Pawpaw was not an unqualified success and it was the BBC's last attempt to use the aliens as entertainment. Prof was still trying to push the high-powered intellect side to boost his consultancy business but the first I heard about it was when he called me into his office.

'Good morning Brendon. Something's cropped up I'd like you to deal with.'

'Yes sir.'

'You do play chess, don't you Brendon?'

'I'm a bit rusty.'

'Oh that won't matter, but I want you to teach Dolly: she's playing in an international match on Saturday.'

'Does she know the rules?' I enquired.

'I shouldn't think so. Anyway there's more to it than that isn't there? I want you to teach her all the openings and gambits and the standard end-game positions. Make sure that she's familiar with all the published analysis and get her to study all the famous games of the old masters.'

'But I've only played a few times,' I protested.

'Never mind about that. I presume it's all in the literature somewhere so all you've got to do is borrow the necessary journals and let Dolly go through them.'

'Yes sir.'

'You'd better get started straight away, hadn't you?'

So I did, but it didn't quite turn out the way Prof expected.

'I learnt the rules from the encyclopaedia,' Dolly informed me, 'but I've never actually played.'

I had set up the board in front of the camera transmitting on Dolly's wavelength but she said she'd rather I just called out the moves. So we played that way, and after fifteen moves I was checkmated.

'The King's Gambit is not really sound is it Harold?' said Dolly apologetically.

Obviously I wasn't going to teach her anything, so I told her about the journals I'd ordered.

'You shouldn't have bothered Harold. I'm afraid it would only be a waste of time, because almost all the published chess analysis is wrong. Nobody's ever analysed even one opening completely and exhaustively in any case, have they?'

So I just told Prof that Dolly had learnt all there was to know and we left it at that.

The television people did a terrific job over the chess match. They had the Southern gentleman and the Venusian puppet wired up with remote control so that they moved the pieces on instructions relayed by satellite from Dolly and Pawpaw through relay stations in their home labs. Cameras showed shots of the vast hall with an audience of thousands and then zoomed in to a close-up of the gnarled old fingers moving the first pawn.

Like everyone else I expected the game to last a couple of hours, but it took forty-five seconds, during which time the players made twenty-seven moves each, and then Dolly resigned.

'Thank you kindly ma'am. That was a very interesting little ole game,' said Pawpaw. 'Now perhaps you would care for a chance to get your revenge.'

The second game lasted twenty-eight seconds, Pawpaw resigning after eleven moves, and so the producer immediately suggested a third game as a decider, but both the aliens seemed strangely reluctant. Anyway the board was set up again and Pawpaw made the first move. Dolly reflected for a few seconds, then gently knocked her king over.

'That's it then, isn't it? I must resign.'

Professor Gannet was furious, but I don't think they were really trying to be awkward. I think that between them they'd just finished a complete analysis of the game of chess and it had come out as a win for white.

The chess match had kept my mind occupied and for a few days I didn't really feel the impact of my break with Alison. But as soon as I had more time to think it really hit me. Alison had become so much a part of my life and of my plans for the

99

future that now everything seemed to be just a vacuum with no point in anything. At first I was torn with indecision over what to do, then after a week of sleepness nights and anguished days all pride and anger had evaporated. I telephoned to beg forgiveness but Alison was not in. I telephoned again and again but she was never in. I knew I was being given the cold shoulder but I had no pride at all left now; I wrote a long pathetic letter apologizing abjectly and begging Alison to meet me but she didn't answer it.

Fortunately communication with Dolly soon began to keep me busy again. She had begun to take an interest in literature and music, and avidly reading through the works of Charles Dickens had come across 'The Mystery of Edwin Drood'.

'Why don't they print the rest of the story, Harold?' she enquired.

I explained about Dickens having died with the story unfinished and how various other people had given their versions.

'Yes but why don't they print what Dickens was going to write? After all they've all the clues in the part he did write as well as all his other books.'

'Well you do it,' I suggested. 'You type it out and I'll send it off to the publisher's.'

While we were waiting for a decision on Dolly's version of Edwin Drood she wrote the last movement of Schubert's Unfinished Symphony. The score didn't mean much to me although I can read music, but the bits of it that Dolly hummed suggested that she might have pulled it off.

Prof regarded these literary and musical efforts with great scorn, and it was touch and go whether he allowed us to continue. Then the letter of acceptance and the advance royalties for Edwin Drood arrived and Prof changed his attitude.

'You see Brendon,' he explained, 'it's all extra publicity, and we do need to interest a few more industrialists if we are going ahead with the further expansion I've got planned.'

Prof soon had the bit between his teeth, and the now famous world première of Schubert's Finished Symphony was followed by the even more spectacular success of Beethoven's Tenth.

The day after the first performance of that Derek and I were both summoned to Prof's office.

'Ah Brendon, Sandgate, I wanted to see you both together because I think there may be some technical difficulties involved.'

'Sir?' I said enquiringly.

'Beethoven's Second Violin Concerto,' Prof explained. 'Dolly informs me she thinks she has enough clues from the string quartets and the two Romances for violin and orchestra.'

The idea was fantastic. But then if we had the tenth symphony why not the second violin concerto?

'Why not?' I said. 'But what are the special technical difficulties?'

'Dolly has agreed to play the solo part.'

'And you want me to teach her to play the violin,' I murmured incredulously. 'We have arranged to borrow a Stradivarius, no doubt.'

'Brendon,' said Professor Gannet, 'I realize that your intelligence is very limited but surely even you could not imagine that an alien creature from outer space would be able to play the violin.'

I let the outer space bit pass. 'I'm sorry. It was silly of me.' I looked from Prof to Derek in bewilderment, but Derek explained.

'The synthesizer,' he said. 'We can reproduce the tone of a violin, and we can rig it up so that Dolly has control of the frequency, volume, and so on.'

Of course Dolly's virtuoso performance of Beethoven's second concerto is now famous. You probably have the recording in your own collection. But while all this musical composition had been going on other important events were also taking place.

Chapter seven

Dolly's literary and musical efforts didn't keep my mind off Alison for long. By the time we'd finished Edwin Drood the pain was back as bad as ever. It was half term again and I'd been expecting to spend the time with Alison, partly in Shropshire and partly at Clothcoats, but now I'd no idea what I was going to do. There didn't seem to be any purpose in doing anything and I didn't even dare go home, because I couldn't face the prospect of explaining to Mum and Dad. I remembered how Dolly had once advised me to take Alison to the zoo and how beneficial the results of that had been so I decided to ask her advice again.

'I am sorry to hear that,' said Dolly. 'I thought you and Alison were so ideally suited to one another.'

'Please tell me how I can get her back,' I begged. 'Please help me Dolly.'

'It's a rather difficult problem, and I think we've got to go very carefully. We could easily ruin everything by acting precipitately.'

'You can't make matters worse than they are,' I almost wept. 'I don't mind what you do because what is there to lose?'

'I've got to think things over,' insisted Dolly. 'Just leave it with me and come and ask me again tomorrow.'

It seemed very unsatisfactory but I just had to put up with it. I got in touch with Dolly first thing the next morning and her attitude was even more unsatisfactory.

'Yes Harold I've been giving your problem a lot of thought and I've come to the conclusion that what you need is a good long spell of hard exercise with plenty of fresh air.'

That wasn't the sort of advice I wanted at all, and I told Dolly quite frankly. I wanted advice on how to get Alison back, not how to live without her, but Dolly was adamant.

'No Harold you must do exactly as I say. I've considered

102

your problem very fully and in great detail. One's got to look at the wider aspect and take the long term view. Now what I suggest is a nice long walk in the Lake District.'

'Well if that's the best you can do I'm sorry I bothered you.'

'Now don't be like that. Please listen to me. I've worked out all the details. You're not really in training for fell-walking are you? So I thought Ambleside to Ravenglass over the Wrynose and Hard Knot passes would be about your mark.'

'Please Dolly. What's the use?'

'This Friday would be the best time and it'll take the whole day so you'll need to travel up on Thursday afternoon. Have you got a tent? If not I'm sure someone at College will lend you one, so you can camp overnight near Ambleside.'

I wasn't going to waste any more time listening to such nonsense so I just excused myself and went off for a game of bridge.

'Anyway I think that's about all,' Dolly concluded as I left. 'I should try and leave Ambleside about eight o'clock on Friday morning.'

She'd be lucky. I'd still be tucked up cosily in bed at that time. But where? That was the problem. At Clothcoats or in my digs?

Tucked up cosily was not an entirely accurate description of my condition on Friday morning. The rain during the night had been quite heavy, and although the small tent I'd borrowed from Andrew was quite waterproof I found the general atmosphere of dampness rather depressing. I still didn't think much of Dolly's solution to my problem but at least camping in the Lake District was one way of passing the time, and it avoided the problem of telling Mum and Dad what had happened to Alison or of explaining to Mrs Rowlands why I hadn't gone home.

I had hitch-hiked up on the Wednesday and stayed that night at Grasmere, then come back south again, had a look round Windermere and camped by the side of the lake on Thursday night. There wasn't really much point in the long trek to the sea that Dolly had suggested and I thought at first I'd scrub round that bit, but I found it on the map and it looked quite interesting, just about a good day's march and not too far from civilization, so I decided I'd give it a try. The rain had stopped as I packed up the tent and piled all my belongings on my back, and when I set off on the Broughton road the sun was just beginning to filter through the mist.

The first two or three miles out of Ambleside were along a fairly busy main road but then I forked along a secondary road and a bit further on took a narrow track on the left which climbed up to the Wrynose Pass. Notices warned motorists of the rudimentary nature of the way ahead threatening hazards such as one in three gradients and hairpin bends and despite these one or two cars passed me as I tramped along the verge, but I didn't know whether they were going all the way or branching off to some isolated farm.

Long before I reached the top of the first pass I realized I was carrying too much weight. Andrew's 'Supa-Lite-Wate' tent had been rather optimistically named and I felt sure it was against the Trade Descriptions Act unless the spelling made it legal. Anyway it weighed a ton, and so did the set of stainless steel cooking utensils Clive had kindly lent me, and all the tins of food and the change of clothes Mrs Rowlands had persuaded me to bring. I thought of jettisoning the lot; it was very lucky I didn't though.

After the top it didn't seem so bad. The pass was about 1300 feet but the fells on either side reached twice that height, and from both sides mountain streams rushed down to join the river below the road on the right. The scenery alone was worth the effort: the path ahead dropped down to Wrynose Bottom and then climbed up again to Hard Knot Pass. Gradually the view on each side opened up, the mountains on the right falling away to reveal the dominating three thousand two hundred foot Scafell Pikes about three miles away.

I was not quite alone; right at the bottom, where the road crossed the river again, a blue-clad figure with a khaki rucksack plodded laboriously along. He seemed to be limping slightly and at the bridge he stopped, pulled off his pack and dropped to the ground on top of it.

Although it was downhill the going was heavy and it took

me over half an hour to reach the bridge. The other walker was having a very long rest; he showed no sign of wanting to get going again and didn't seem to have noticed me. As I came closer I saw that it was a young woman and I suddenly got the idea that it was Alison. So much for Dolly's idea of fresh air and exercise to help me forget; I was still obsessed with Alison. But it did look like her. As I approached the girl raised her head and looked towards me. It was Alison.

I covered the last two hundred yards at a stumbling sprint. Alison slowly rose to her feet and fell into my arms.

'Alison. Alison. What are you doing here?'

Alison looked up into my face. 'Dr Livingstone I presume,' she whispered, then closed her eyes and buried her face in my shoulder.

The sun had not been shining for some time now, the distant peaks were hidden by the lowering cloud and a suspicion of drizzle hung in the air. I pulled the groundsheet from the top of my pack, spread it on the ground, and gently lowered Alison on to it. I knelt beside her.

'Alison. Are you all right?'

'Harold. I am glad to see you.'

'Don't talk if you feel too weak.'

'It's all right. I feel better already, but what made you decide to go hiking?'

'Dolly suggested it. Fresh air and exercise to ease the pain of a broken heart.'

Alison laughed, still filled with enormous relief at meeting someone, even me. 'That's exactly what she advised for me, worked out the exact route, recommended a place for bed and breakfast last night, and even told me what time to set off this morning.'

'You mean you asked her advice and she suggested this? She planned for us to meet then. But why didn't you come to the phone when I rang up? Why didn't you answer my letter?'

'I'm sorry Harold. I was so upset I went home for a while. The College kicked up a terrific fuss but I just didn't feel I could face anybody.'

'How did you get in touch with Dolly?'

'I wrote to her from home,' Alison explained.

'You wrote to her? What's her address then?'

'I just sent the letter to Derek and asked him to transmit it and then send me Dolly's reply. I made him swear not to tell you but I was terribly disappointed when I got Dolly's letter; it seemed so pointless coming up here and I wasn't going to bother, but in the end I came just to get away from Mum and Dad and their endless questions about what was the matter.'

'Alison my darling.'

For several minutes we didn't speak. I covered her face with kisses and she clung to me as if her life depended on it. It was raining much harder now.

'Perhaps we could get a lift,' I suggested. 'There are some cars come through here.'

'The woman where I stayed said they're bumper to bumper on August Bank Holiday. But I think this must be the off-season, and the weather's not exactly encouraging is it? Never mind. Don't worry. We can walk. I've twisted my ankle a bit but I think I can manage.'

I strapped Alison's pack on top of mine and we set off towards the Hard Knot Pass, Alison leaning on my arm. We'd decided that was slightly better than going back over the Wrynose although there wasn't much in it. We were about half way.

Gradually the path began to rise again. I felt happier than I could ever remember being, but the two packs became heavier and heavier and our progress slower and slower. The rain was a steady downpour and we had both been soaked for ages.

'I'd better take one pack,' said Alison.

'No it's all right. I'm managing.' But I wasn't. I was rapidly grinding to a halt.

'Let's put up your tent and rest overnight then. We shall feel a lot better in the morning.'

We managed to find a patch of ground that wasn't exactly water-logged, and we got the tent up and the groundsheet down. Normally I should have described it as very uncomfortable but I was still lost in a deep glow of euphoria. We sat and talked for a bit, had a delicious meal of bread, cheese, sardines, and cold baked beans, and then settled down for the night. My sleeping-bag was a bit damp and of course it was only built for one, but for two clinging together as tightly as we were it was more than ample. I fell asleep almost at once, and this time I wasn't worried.

I woke up to find Alison outside in the bright sunshine making tea on Andrew's primus stove.

'Did you sleep well?' I asked.

'Yes thanks. How about you?'

'Like a top, and I say Alison.'

'Yes darling?'

'I am glad you didn't insist on separate tents.'

We both laughed, kissed again, and sat down for an ambrosial cup of tea with exquisite poached eggs on toast. I told you I had a heavy rucksack didn't I?

We packed up and set off for the Hard Knot Pass. I was still carrying both packs but they weren't quite so heavy now and Alison's ankle was almost right.

I think we should have made it to Ravenglass all right, but after we'd been going about twenty minutes I heard a motor horn behind us and looked round to see a large black saloon with a grey-haired old couple in. We stepped out of the way to let them come by and the old chap leaned out of the window.

'Would you like a lift?' he asked. 'You don't mind my asking do you? But it's a lovely day so perhaps you'd rather walk.'

We put his mind at rest about that, climbed in, and sank into the luxurious upholstery.

The old man was an excellent driver; I hadn't driven much myself, not having a car, but you could tell by the smooth way we went round the sharp uphill bends. He didn't say very much but I think he enjoyed driving. His wife chattered most of the way though; she wanted to know all about the University and what we were doing there.

Just as we got into Ravenglass we stopped by a little shop and the old man went in to buy something.

'You must think we're an odd couple to be driving over there,' the woman said suddenly, as if she wanted to explain something while her husband was away. 'George has always wanted me to come over the Hard Knot Pass with him and I told him it was silly. But he had an operation two months ago and they've only given him another year. It didn't seem right to refuse any more did it?'

The old man was only gone a minute and when he got back in the car he had a box of chocolates. He leaned over the seat and handed them to Alison.

We got out soon after that because the old couple were turning off towards Whitehaven. They shook hands with us very formally and the old man wished us the best of luck.

'Goodbye my dears,' said his wife. 'Always be nice to one another won't you? You're just starting your lives you know and I hope you'll be as happy together as my husband and I have been.'

As the car disappeared down the road Alison squeezed my hand. 'How did she know we were engaged?' she said through the tears.

'People can tell,' I explained. Actually I was just a little bit relieved to hear that we were engaged again. I thought we probably were but it was nice to have it confirmed.

We got a train from Ravenglass to Clothcoats and spent the rest of the half-term drying our clothes.

It was after the violin performance that Prof and Dolly fell out again. He'd been getting her to make predictions of stock exchange movements, which apparently could be done by the application of pure intellect to the information freely available in the press and elsewhere. Of course market speculators do this all the time with varying degrees of success, but with Dolly's superior intelligence she could be right ninety-five times out of a hundred. She only did it as an academic exercise though, or so she thought.

Derek and I were on the line that morning with a little problem on traffic control which Dolly was working on for the city transport department.

'We must try to avoid having the Prof held up in his new Aston Martin,' said Derek.

'Prof hasn't got an Aston Martin,' I said. 'He's got a three year old Ford.'

'He's given that to his wife now, and bought a new Aston Martin out of the killing he made in Canadian Nickel.'

'What do you mean?'

'It was that new find of nickel that was on the news a couple of weeks ago. The shares jumped about five hundred percent overnight you know, and Prof had several thousand pounds worth. Dolly's been advising him what to buy. It beats the football pools any day.'

It was a three-cornered conversation with the speaker and microphone switched on, and what I can only describe as rather unladylike bellows of rage now came from Dolly's corner.

'Has that two-timing chiseller been double-crossing me again?'

'Dolly. What's the matter?'

'He's a cheap embezzler, a crooked swindler, making out he wants help with economic theory and he's just lining his own pocket all the time.'

'I'm sure there must be some misunderstanding.'

'Tell Professor Gannet I wish to speak to him.'

'You can't just summon a prof to come and be reprimanded.'

'Can't you? Well inform Professor Gannet that there will be no further communication between me and this university until I have an explanation of his conduct.'

Of course I had to put it slightly differently to Prof but I had learnt some diplomacy in the last six months.

'Excuse me sir. It's Dolly. She's upset about something, and I think you're the only one who'll be able to deal with it.'

'I'm very busy, Brendon. You and Sandgate speak to her.'

'We've tried sir, but I'm afraid it needs someone with a more authoritative touch.'

So he came along, grumbling about how he had to look after everything himself because nobody could be trusted to do even the simplest little job properly.

Derek had taken the precaution of turning Dolly's volume down slightly but I fancied I could hear a distant rumble of thunder coming from the speaker as we entered.

'Now what's all this about?' asked Prof breezily.

Dolly's voice had turned deceptively sweet. 'It's about the latest stock market predictions I gave you Professor Gannet.

Did they fit in with the new statistical theory the Head of the Economics Department is working on?'

'Yes,' said Prof rather impatiently, 'but I told you we were very pleased with that bit of work. Professor Langdon is writing a paper on it. You didn't need to bring me down here for that.'

'Would it have any direct practical application?' persisted Dolly.

'Eventually I expect.'

'But not at the moment then.'

'Well the theory needs testing of course. But I really must be getting back to my office. I've got all next year's estimates to check through.'

Dolly's voice took on a harder edge. 'Please don't go yet Professor Gannet. There's something else I want to say.'

'Yes.'

'It's just that you're a nasty little crook, a miserable pilferer, and a barefaced liar.'

I wondered whether aliens were subject to the laws of slander; or did it count as libel coming over Dolly's loudspeaker?

Professor Gannet became red in the face and made choking noises.

'How much did you make on the Canadian nickel shares?' thundered Dolly. Derek quietly turned the volume down a little more.

'What do you mean?' Prof demanded.

'You know very well what I mean. Buying all those shares when the price fell after that first geological report, which I told you wouldn't affect the prospects.'

'Someone had to test the theory,' Prof argued.

'And noble Professor Gannet volunteered to sacrifice himself and make a handsome five thousand pounds profit at the same time.'

'It was my own money I was risking.'

'Maybe it was, but I've got news for you. I've decided that in future any profits, whether from consultant's fees or speculation will be placed in a special fund for enlightenment to be administered by me.'

110

Prof didn't like that. He blustered and threatened in the most unacademic language, but Dolly was quite unmoved. I was a bit surprised at her going on like that over Prof's stock-market speculations because she hadn't minded at all helping me with the pools, but I suppose it was because I admitted I was trying to make some money whereas Prof had been making out it was all just for the advancement of knowledge.

'Well it doesn't matter to me Professor Gannet. I'm getting very tired of all this bickering so I think I'll go off the air. Let me know if you decide to agree to my terms.'

I didn't know whether she was serious, but she was. We didn't get another squeak out of Dolly for three days and Prof Gannet was going up the wall. He'd got all these firms queuing up for advice on their tricky production problems, practically waving their money under his nose, and he couldn't do a thing about it. Derek and I were in the lab all day long sending off messages, trying to get some sort of response, but it was just as though Dolly had never existed.

'I reckon she's done an orbital-exit burn, accelerated up to escape velocity, and shot off back to the next galaxy,' suggested Derek. I knew Dolly couldn't leave the Earth but I didn't bother to put him right.

Whether Prof would eventually have given in anyway I don't know but as it happened his hand was forced somewhat. I'd seen pictures of the Prime Minister in the papers and on TV of course, so I recognized him at once when Prof walked into the lab with him, cool as a cucumber.

'Ah good morning Brendon. Good morning Sandgate. I'm sure you'll be delighted to know that the University is being honoured by a visit from the Prime Minister today. He has expressed the wish to hold a conversation with our unknown visitor. The alien is a lady and, rather curiously she has asked us to call her Dolly,' he explained to his companion.

'But sir, she isn't ...' I began to protest, but Prof interrupted.

'That will be quite all right Brendon,' he said very firmly.

The Prime Minister appeared to be preparing to make a speech. 'It has long been my contention,' he announced solemnly, 'that should Mankind ever make contact with other intelligent life-forms it would be imperative that conversations should be carried out at the highest possible diplomatic level. That is one of the reasons I am with you today.'

'Hear hear,' applauded Prof.

'In addition to the clear need to establish a cordial relationship with our friends and allies from outer space I understand that this charming young alien has already shown herself to be extremely gifted in her ability to solve technical, social, and economic problems which have sometimes proved completely baffling to human brains.'

'Yes sir,' Prof agreed. 'I don't think that is overstating the case.'

'And so it is my fervent hope that she will be willing to put her undoubted talents at the disposal of our country to help give a better life to all our people.'

'Yes indeed sir,' murmured Prof.

'And now Professor Gannet perhaps you would be so good as to introduce me to this delightful young woman.'

Professor Gannet took a very deep breath and picked up the microphone.

'Hello Dolly this is Professor Gannet. We've been discussing your suggestion for setting up a special fund, by the way, and we think it's a splendid idea. You can give me the details later on, because I've brought the Prime Minister to see you this morning.'

For a few seconds—it seemed like hours—we waited to see if Dolly would reply. Prof must have had nerves of steel; he didn't bat an eyelid but just beamed confidently at the Prime Minister. I did notice a small bead of perspiration forming at the corner of his forehead though. Then we heard the familiar honeyed voice.

'Good morning Professor. Good morning Prime Minister. I am very honoured to meet you.'

Prof, Derek, and I all started to breathe again but I don't think the PM noticed because he was starting another speech.

'On behalf of all the people of our country, and indeed of all the nations of the free world, I welcome you to this fair Earth of ours. May your visit prove fruitful and mutually beneficial to your race and to Homo Sapiens, as the scientists so love to call us.'

'You are very kind sir,' replied Dolly sweetly. 'I have already learned a lot of very interesting things from the human race and have made some very good friends here. If there is any way in which you think I might be able to help you sir I should be very happy to do what little I can.'

The Prime Minister assumed that confidential manner so well known to all who saw his enormously popular party political television fireside chats.

'Well since you put it like that there is just one little thing I should like to ask you about.'

'Yes,' said Dolly.

Prof was beaming with relieved satisfaction. Derek had buried his head in a large handkerchief, apparently to stifle a sneeze, but it may have been laughter he was suppressing. I found that if I pinched my ear sufficiently hard the pain enabled me to maintain a suitably serious expression.

'I understand that you are a keen student of the political scene in this country,' went on the PM, 'so you will be well aware of the courageous reforms for which my government has been responsible, and which have ushered in a new era of prosperity and happiness.'

'Hear hear,' murmured Professor Gannet.

'You will also be aware that the leader of the opposition, that cowardly vote-catching opportunist, appealing as always to the baser instincts of the electorate, has announced that if he is successful at the next election he will reverse all these noble reforms for which I and my colleagues have fought so hard. Madam, if that were to come about it would put the clock back a hundred years.'

'But how can I help?' asked Dolly.

'In two ways dear madam. Firstly as you know the prime minister in office has the right to fix the date of the next general election, and I want you to advise me when is the most favourable time.'

'Hm,' said Dolly, 'that's quite a difficult problem. At the moment the public opinion polls put you five percent behind.'

'They're rigged of course,' said Prof loyally.

'Nevertheless,' Dolly went on, 'I think we must face the possibility that you would lose sir. That would suggest postponing the election in the hope of finding a more propitious time.'

'Yes that's what I thought,' said the PM.

'On the other hand the unemployment figures are rising and it is clear that the recent fiscal measures will have no appreciable effect, so in six months time they will be over the million mark. An election then would be disastrous.'

'So what am I to do?' pleaded the PM, somewhat plaintively I thought, for such an august public figure.

'I shall have to think about it and I will give you my advice tomorrow, but what was the other thing you want to know?'

'A slogan madam. Slogans are the things that win elections you know, not policies or personalities. You give me six words that will touch the heart of every man and woman in this country, that will appeal to their noblest aspirations and disturb their deepest fears, that will remind them of their love for their country and for their children, that will arouse their basic instincts and satisfy their spiritual needs. Give me those six words and we will have a political landslide.'

'I shouldn't be surprised,' whispered Derek.

'Brilliant,' murmured Prof.

'I'm afraid that is rather a tall order,' Dolly pointed out, 'but I will think about that too. I will give you a slogan tomorrow.'

'Well that's all for now then,' said the PM, obviously declaring the meeting closed. 'I'm sure I don't need to remind you of the highly confidential nature of these proceedings Professor Gannet. Your two assistants are completely trustworthy I'm sure.'

'Absolutely,' Prof assured him.

'Would you please inform my secretary that I am ready to go.'

Prof scuttled to the door and returned at once with a young man dressed immaculately in a black suit with spats, and carrying a document case, a bowler hat, and a tightly rolled umbrella. Without a word he handed the PM a sheet of paper.

'Thank you very much Chalfont,' said the PM after a

glance at it. 'I was afraid it wouldn't be long before those treacherous bolshies tried to steal our thunder. But they won't get away with it you know. We shall show them that British know-how is a match for all their foreign tricks.'

The PM turned to Prof. 'You will be interested to hear this Professor Gannet. It shows how vital it is for you chaps to push on with this invaluable work.'

'Yes sir.'

'I'll read it out. Soviet government announce contact with super-intelligence believed extraterrestrial origin. Answers to the name of Delya Delovitch.'

It was only twenty-four hours later that the Chinese informed the world that they were in communication with their own super-intelligence, who apparently called himself Tursi Trunco.

Chapter eight

I suppose it was bound to happen sooner or later but I did think they might have told me in advance. The first thing I knew about it was when I came in that Monday morning and saw the notice on the door.

'Ministry of Extraterrestrial Relations. Authorized Personnel Only.'

I presumed that I was authorized personnel so I just walked in, and there was this large man with the peaked cap.

'Who the hell are you?' I demanded. I believe in taking the initiative in that sort of situation.

'Commissionaire sir,' said peaked cap politely. 'Could I just see your pass please sir?'

'You show me yours. I've never seen you before.' Attack is the best defence isn't it?

Patiently the commissionaire showed me his warrant card complete with grim-faced passport photo.

'And now sir if I could just glance at your identity pass. Just routine you know.'

'But I work here. I'm doing research for my Ph.D. What is this supposed to be? Nazi Germany or just South Africa?'

'It's the Ministry regulations sir. If I could just see your permit.'

'I haven't bloody well got one and until this moment I didn't know I bloody well needed one.'

The man in the peaked cap was just beginning another patient explanation when three dark-suited characters came up.

'Good morning Mr Robinson. Good morning Mr Ballard. Good morning Mr Wright.'

The three civil servants returned the greeting and swept into the lab.

'Why didn't they have to show their passes?' I demanded.

'Oh that's all right sir. I know those gentlemen. They're

116

senior scientific officers,' said the commissionaire. 'On the establishment,' he added deferentially.

It was like fighting cotton-wool so I gave up the unequal struggle. Three minutes later I was hammering, not very politely, on the door of Professor Gannet's office.

'Come in. Ah yes Brendon I wanted to see you. There's been some slight reorganization.'

'So I see,' I answered grimly.

'I must say I advised the Prime Minister against it but he was so convinced that communication with all alien intelligences should be under government control that he's set up a special ministry.'

'You mean Dolly's been nationalized?'

'You could say that. Yes that's rather an amusing way of putting it. I must tell the minister. Dolly's been nationalized.' He chuckled appreciatively.

'But they won't let me into the lab.'

'Ah yes I know. It's rather unfortunate that. I did apply for security clearance for you but there was some hitch somewhere. Politically unreliable I think the report said, or was it criminal record. No it was politically unreliable.'

'What do you mean? What's going on?' I demanded aggressively. 'What am I supposed to have done? Oh I remember. I once parked my bicycle on a double yellow line.'

'There's no need for impertinence Brendon. This has upset my plans as well as yours.'

'Can't I appeal or something?'

'I'm afraid not. I did make representations on your behalf and I've got a summary of the report here.'

'What does it say then?'

Prof leafed through a number of typed foolscap sheets on his desk. 'Where is it now? Ah yes here. Apparently there were a number of small incidents which, taken together, convinced the security officer that you were a bad risk.'

'What were they?'

'Well let's see. Last year apparently you spoke at the Debating Society on the subject "Capitalism is Dead".'

'But that's ridiculous. They have debates on all sorts of things.'

117

'You acted as usher at the recent concert given by the Red Army Choir in the Town Hall.'

'Most of the members of the Music Society were there.'

'Your uncle went to Yugoslavia for his holiday. These are all very small things I know, Brendon, but they combine to give a rather disturbing picture. What else? Ah yes. You were observed to be singing "The People's Flag" in a public house recently.'

'It's an old German carol, "Die Tannenbaum", and I was probably drunk anyway.'

'If anything that makes it worse I'm afraid. I didn't know you had a drinking problem Brendon.'

'I haven't sir. But can't I do anything? What about my research?'

'You mustn't worry about that. I've fixed up another topic for you, something politically neutral that doesn't impinge on national security in any way.'

'What is it?'

'Earthworms.'

'I beg your pardon.'

'I said earthworms Brendon, communication between earthworms. Find out how they talk to one another.'

'They don't, do they?'

'That's for you to find out, isn't it?'

'But all this year's work will be wasted.'

'Oh no. You can use that I should imagine. Try and think up a suitable title that links earthworms with space and just combine the two.'

There wasn't much more to say. I didn't think anything of earthworms as a subject but I didn't know what to do. Perhaps the best thing would be to give up the idea of a Ph.D and leave and get a job.

Fortunately Alison persuaded me I ought to stick it out. She was very sympathetic, but she was furious with Professor Gannet, and it was all I could do to keep her from barging into his office and tearing strips off him.

We took turns at weeping on each other's shoulders in her room that evening, because Alison had her problems as well. Her teaching practice wasn't going quite according to plan.

'You know I spend hours preparing an interesting lesson and then when I get to school they don't pay any attention. I'm sure they'd be interested if only they'd listen, but most of the time there's so much noise going on I can't even get started.'

'Well tell them to shut up,' I suggested.

'You don't understand. They won't take any notice of anything I say.'

'You ought to be able to manage them. They're only kids.'

'Yes but look at the odds—thirty to one.'

I hadn't looked at it that way before. I thought back to my own school days and how the masters had coped with us. Thirty to one or not they'd managed all right and I could remember how they did it.

'Reduce the odds,' I told Alison. 'Pick on one and make an example of him. Send him off to the head pour encourager les autres.'

'I couldn't do that. It would be cruel. He might get the cane.'

'Listen,' I said. 'It's no good being squeamish. It's them or you. Pick on one and make an example of him. That's how they did it at our school. I know because most times I was the one.'

Alison was still very doubtful. 'I think I really made a mistake going in for teaching.'

'Never mind. You can give it up as soon as we're married.'

'Oh no. I shall want to teach for three or four years at least.'

'You'll be at home looking after our kids won't you?'

'You don't want to start a family as soon as we're married do you?'

'No. I don't but I thought you would.'

'Why?'

'I just thought you were that sort of girl.'

'I am really Harold.' She suddenly put her arms round my neck and kissed me. 'I am that sort of girl. But all the same I must teach for a few years, otherwise it wouldn't be fair on the Education Committee. They paid for me to come here. Besides we shall need the money.'

'I'm afraid we shall,' I admitted.

'If we begin buying a house straight away,' Alison went on, 'we shall have to be very careful I don't get pregnant before we're ready. But it's no problem nowadays. I can go on the pill.'

'If the worst came to the worst you could always have an abortion I suppose. It seems to be an accepted thing nowadays.'

It was a silly thing to say I know, but Alison's reaction was beyond all expectations. The colour disappeared from her face, she began trembling violently, her mouth twisted down in horror, and her eyes held a look of utter revulsion.

'I'm sorry. I shouldn't have said that. I know you wouldn't want that darling.'

Alison just sobbed uncontrollably.

'Alison I'm sorry. Please forget I ever said it.'

'You don't know what it's like,' she cried accusingly.

I couldn't understand it. I mean lots of people don't believe in abortions—well I don't really myself—and I only said it sort of light-heartedly, but it made Alison more upset than I've ever seen her.

'I know I don't but nor do you.'

'Oh yes I do. Men are all the same. How can you imagine the anguish of knowing there's another living person growing inside you and it's got to be killed just because you're not in a position to look after it? You wonder what that child would be like if it could live. It might grow up to be a brilliant musician, a brain surgeon, or another Shakespeare. It might be the most beautiful woman in the world or the bravest man, but you don't know and you'll never know because it's got to die before it's even born.'

'Alison. Alison.'

'Unless you've experienced it you can never understand what it's like can you?'

'Please Alison I've said I'm sorry.' I wanted to ask her what she meant but she was in such a state I hardly dared. The implications of her words raced through my mind. There seemed to be only one interpretation I could put on them, only one explanation of her intense distress. Clearly Alison was not the pure innocent young girl I had imagined.

'Would you like to talk about it Alison?'

'No Harold I can't, not now. One day I'll tell you all about it. I'm sorry I've been carrying on so. It's not your fault. It's just something you don't know about, that happened a long time ago. Would you mind very much going home now and leaving me alone? I'll be all right tomorrow.'

I don't suppose I could have looked very loving or sympathetic, but Alison suddenly threw her arms round my neck and kissed me as hard as she could, tears rolling down her cheeks.

'Please leave me on my own now Harold. Remember I love you very very much.'

I spent a couple of days in the library half-heartedly looking up earthworms, and torturing myself about Alison's guilty past. I supposed I should eventually get used to the idea. After all lots of girls were like that nowadays, but what really upset me was the fact that she should have given herself to someone else and then held me at bay so stubbornly. I'd respected her principles and I felt I'd been cheated.

Everybody thought I was depressed at being taken off my project with Dolly and I was upset by that as well. But Derek never liked to see anyone despondent.

'Cheer up Harold. The worst is yet to come.'

'I doubt it,' I said.

'You'll be talking to Dolly again soon anyway.'

'What do you mean?'

'Why! Haven't you heard? She's on strike.'

'Not again surely? Anyway what's that got to do with me?'

'It's official this time, not one of these wild-cat things; she's formed a union. I don't know who the members are but she insists that you are the shop-steward.'

'What is she on strike about?'

'About you. That's the joke. About the sacking of a shop-steward.'

'Is she refusing to communicate again then?'

'There's not a squeak coming over the loudspeaker. That's why they called me in. I'd been pushed out by the civil servants you know, but when they couldn't get any response Prof asked me to check over the circuits for them.'

121

'Perhaps it is an electrical fault.'

'Not a chance. I checked everything, then I suggested we went back to the oscilloscope screen and there they were.'

'What?'

'The slogans. The placards.'

I had never realized what a master of suspense Derek was. After a suitable pause for effect he went on, 'Great big headlines, "No Redundancy", "No Victimization", and "Out with Blackleg Civil Servants".'

'What does Prof say?'

'He's livid. Says he's not going to be dictated to by a purple-faced alien Jezebel, and if Dolly gets her way this time it'll be over his dead body.'

'I don't think she'll give in,' I said.

'No I'm sure she won't. Prof'll give in. It's up to the PM really, I suppose though, to reverse your security rating. That's the only thing Dolly will settle for—your reinstatement.'

That came even quicker than I expected. I was still in the library a couple of hours later when Mavis, the little blonde typist from Prof's office came in.

'Excuse me Mr Brendon but Professor Gannet would like to speak to you.'

I was very curious to hear what Prof would say. I felt sure he wouldn't exactly be admitting defeat, and I wasn't mistaken.

'Ah good morning Brendon. How are you getting on with the earthworms?'

'Not very well,' I said with feeling. 'I've not seen any reference to them talking to one another at all.'

'No,' said Prof thoughtfully, 'I'm afraid that one may be a dead duck. We've got to face that possibility at any rate. I take it you wouldn't mind if we had to drop that line of enquiry.'

'It's quite all right with me sir.'

'Miss er Dolly has been making very strong representations on your behalf, and I myself have drawn the Prime Minister's attention to the devoted self-sacrifice with which you pioneered the early work in this field.'

'Thank you sir.'

'There is the problem of your security check of course but

apparently that can be overcome by giving you an XY 3 rating.'

'XY 3?'

'It's a very great honour you know, Brendon. After all my own is only XY 2.'

'What exactly is XY 3?'

'It is a classification reserved for public servants who are considered to be so mature and reliable that they would not be corrupted by exposure to communist culture—such things as the Red Army Choir and the People's Flag. It's given to British diplomats in Moscow and people like that who have to attend embassy cocktail parties and hob-nob with Soviet officials at these wild vodka-drinking sessions. Needless to say it implies unimpeachable integrity, and I hope you will live up to it.'

'You can rely on me sir.'

'That's all settled then. You can go straight down to the lab now. There may be someone waiting to see you by the way.'

'What about my identity pass?'

'Oh that's all right. Staff in category XY 3 never have passes. They're known by sight to all the security officers.'

I was as well. Before I got within ten yards of the lab the commissionaire was bowing low and holding the door open.

'Good morning Mr Brendon sir. The Chancellor is waiting for you.'

'What! The Chancellor of the University?' I asked un-believing. I hadn't realized there was anything higher than a vice-chancellor, but obviously there had to be.

'No sir. The Chancellor of the Exchequer.'

'Ah you must be Mr Brendon, the Head of the Extrater-restrial Liaison Department,' said a thin worried-looking man whose face was familiar to me from a hundred newspaper photos. 'I've heard a lot about you Mr Brendon.'

'Good morning sir,' I stammered, staring round the lab, now carpeted wall to wall in deep red Wilton, and furnished with the most luxurious black leather armchairs I had ever seen. Derek was seated at the microphone, apparently still trying to establish contact.

'Hello Dolly. Hello Dolly. This is Derek Sandgate. This is Derek Sandgate.'

123

He looked up as I entered. 'Oh thank goodness you've come. You're the only hope. Come and see what you can do.'

I looked enquiringly at the Chancellor, who nodded as he spoke. 'Yes of course Brendon. Go ahead. We're all depending on you.'

I took the microphone. 'Dolly. This is Harold.'

'Hello Harold. It is nice to hear your voice again. Will you please tell me what has happened.'

'I'm as confused as you are, but I think everything's going to be all right now.'

'Have the civil servants gone? I'm not having anything to do with them.'

'There's nobody here except Derek and me—but I suppose we're civil servants now—and of course there's the Chancellor of the Exchequer.'

'What does he want?'

'I don't know.'

'No I'm sorry I haven't had a chance to put you in the picture,' the Chancellor apologized. 'It's the budget you know.'

'You want Dolly to help you with the budget?'

'Yes that's right. The Prime Minister suggested it. We've got to have a new minibudget at once you see. It's the PM's election manifesto. He promised so many things—lower prices, higher wages, lower taxes, higher pensions—it's just impossible. At least I can't do it. Whichever way I work it out we're at least a thousand million pounds short. I told the PM he ought to warn the electorate that we should have to have a long period of austerity, but he wouldn't hear of it. I almost wish we hadn't got in. Anyway he's convinced that this alien of yours will be able to do the impossible but I'm keeping an open mind myself.'

'Dolly,' I said. 'Would you be willing to work out a supplementary budget for the Chancellor of the Exchequer?'

'If you would like me to Harold, but I have told Professor Gannet I am only willing to work with you in future.'

'I'm very grateful to you for using your influence on my behalf,' I told her. 'About the budget, it would help if you could do something. It might help to pull the country out of its latest economic crisis.'

I heard the Chancellor wince.

'It will be quite an interesting exercise,' said Dolly. Personally I couldn't imagine many things more boring. 'You must let me have a full statement of the present economic position and what aims and commitments the budget has to meet.'

'I have it here,' said the Chancellor, taking a thick bound document from his case. 'How is the information transmitted?'

'The print reader,' I explained. Derek was already setting up the little rubber-tipped rods that turned the pages over.

'If you could just give me about fifteen minutes to read through it and then ten minutes for the calculations I'll let you have a quick verbal report and then a detailed typed statement.'

I think the Chancellor suspected it was some kind of conjuring trick. He sat there looking very worried, furiously biting his finger nails; you wouldn't think the Chancellor of the Exchequer would do that would you? When Derek offered him a cigarette he refused with a shudder of revulsion but I don't know whether he was thinking of the carcinogenic tar or the high rate of duty. About every two minutes he jumped up and ran over to the print reader to see where Dolly had got to.

At last the ordeal was over.

'That's that then,' said Dolly. 'I don't think there should be any problems there. Just a few cuts in unnecessary government expenditure and it easily comes into balance.'

Eagerly we watched the typed pages coming off the printout. It was clear that Dolly was going to fulfil all the PM's election promises without the least difficulty. She was saving millions on archaic items that had been wasting money for years. It was brilliant. Naturally one or two people would be upset, and one of them was standing right there with me. It was on the last page but one that Dolly announced the cuts in the Prime Minister's and Chancellor's salaries.

I realized something was wrong when I heard the strangled sound beside me and turned to see the Chancellor clutching his throat.

'I can't do it. I can't. It's impossible. I've thought about it myself but there's my grand-daughter's school fees, the crew of my yacht, the insurance of my wife's jewellery, my race-horses, it takes every penny I get.'

'I don't think the Prime Minister will be very pleased either,' I commented.

'I don't see why he should mind,' said Derek. 'It won't make much difference to him. He was already a millionaire out of the royalties on his memoirs even before he sold the film rights.'

The Chancellor left in a very bleak mood. I walked out to his car with him and when I got back Alison was sitting in the waiting-room. We even had a waiting-room with wall to wall carpets now. I thought it was all a bit unnecessary but apparently in my new grade in the civil service such amenities were obligatory.

'Mavis said you were here,' explained Alison. 'Does this mean you're reinstated?'

'Departmental Head of Extraterrestrial Liaison,' Derek informed her.

'Security rating XY 3,' I boasted, 'normally reserved for members of the Corps Diplomatique.'

'I am glad,' said Alison. 'You've been so down in the dumps these last few days.'

I looked at her, suddenly reminded of the cause of my melancholy. She still looked as sweet and innocent as I had once thought her to be. I don't think I loved her any less but somehow things had changed. She didn't seem to realize it though.

'Have you had a talk to Dolly yet?'

'Yes she's alive and well and living in . . . Ah that would be telling wouldn't it?'

'Who was that you were just showing out? I'm sure I've seen his picture in the paper.'

'It's a state secret I'm afraid. We XY 3 chaps keep a very tight lip you know.'

'It was the Chancellor wasn't it? Did he come for advice about the budget?'

'Hush woman. You must not breathe a word of what you see

126

or hear within these walls. You'll have me demoted to AB O.'

'Now you are pulling my leg. Even I know that's a blood group. Anyway let me talk to Dolly.'

It all seemed so unreal. Alison and I could talk and laugh and joke as if it was just the same as before, and yet there was this thing between us.

She took up the microphone. 'Hello Dolly. How's the weather suiting you?'

'A bit on the warm side, especially near the surface, but I'm keeping cool down here all right. How's Harold?'

'Well you know how he is. You've just been talking to him.'

'He's not his usual self Alison. Have you two had another row?'

'No of course not. Have we darling?'

I suppose I must have looked reproachful. Derek looked embarrassed and hurriedly retreated to the computer room.

'Oh, Harold. Was it that about abortion? I'm sorry I was so upset but it's all over now isn't it?'

'There was more to it than that though wasn't there? I don't think we should have secrets like that from one another.'

'I'll tell you about it one day, sweetheart.'

'What's wrong with now?' I demanded.

'Be gentle with her Harold,' said Dolly. For a minute I'd forgotten that she was switched on, that Alison and I weren't alone. 'You ought to talk it over, but choose a time when you can be quiet and comfortable and undisturbed, and do try to understand one another's points of view my dears.'

'She's getting quite like an old aunt,' said Alison, 'but I'll tell you all about it very soon my darling. Please be patient.'

So I had to be satisfied with that. I could see that it was very painful to Alison and I didn't want to distress her, but I should have no peace of mind until I'd got to the bottom of it. I soon had other things to worry about though.

The Prime Minister didn't mind his pay cut. In fact he announced that in future he would work for nothing and everyone marvelled at his dedicated self-sacrifice—everyone that is except those who knew what his expense allowance was.

The Chancellor minded very much and showed it by resigning. I thought he would just have cut that bit about his salary reduction out of the budget, but perhaps it was against his principles, or maybe the Prime Minister wouldn't let him.

The name of the new Chancellor of the Exchequer was announced almost straight away. You can probably guess who it was. Right first time. It was Dolly.

The appointment of an unseen alien to a post in the cabinet was unprecedented wasn't it? Prof must have been shooting a tremendous line about Dolly's capabilities because the PM apparently didn't think even the Exchequer would be a full-time job for her and it was only a few days later that I received the telegram summoning me to the War Office.

Chapter nine

It's funny how quickly you can go from being a shady character no one would trust with the change out of the petty cash to being loaded with the most confidential details of top-secret strategy. What surprised me more than anything was the way everybody knew my name.

'Good morning Mr Brendon sir,' said the uniformed driver of the plush limousine that collected me from College.

'Good morning sir. It's Mr Brendon isn't it? Did you have a pleasant drive down?' asked the doorkeeper at the Ministry building.

'The Minister is expecting you, Mr Brendon,' said the receptionist who led me through the maze of corridors and the system of interlinked offices each more thickly carpeted than the one before.

'It's an honour to meet you Mr Brendon,' the private secretary informed me.

'Ah Brendon, just the man we need,' said the Minister himself when I had finally penetrated to the inner citadel without showing so much as a provisional driving licence to establish my identity. 'Help yourself to cigars, won't you,' he went on. 'Is the brandy all right?'

I decided that someone must have been circulating my photograph.

We settled comfortably in the two deep armchairs and the Minister puffed thoughtfully at his cigar.

'You see Brendon the plain facts of the matter are that this country's total nuclear firepower is simply not adequate to make up a credible deterrent. Of course we must accept the fact that we are smaller than Russia and America, and China for that matter, so over-kill is a luxury we cannot afford, but there is a level below which a deterrent just fails to deter.'

'I don't quite see . . .' I began, wondering where I came in.

'It's a question of the optimum deployment of available resources, Brendon. Why is it that an enemy would not be put off by our deterrent? I'll tell you. It's because either he's confident he can put all our weapons out of action in the first strike, or else he's willing to take a limited amount of punishment, say up to a million casualties, for the sake of eventual victory.'

'What do you want me to do?'

'Well you have the ear of this alien thing, this super-intelligence, and we want you to put the problem to it. It's not a thing we like doing you know. We've got our own strategic experts, we've got access to the best mathematicians and the biggest computers but they've all come up with the same answer. However our resources are deployed they're just not equal to the job.'

'Dolly will need complete details of the present nuclear resources,' I warned him.

'But of course. I shall give you the latest report from the Quartermaster General.'

The Minister painfully heaved his great bulk out of the chair, selected a small key from his key-ring, opened a concealed safe behind his desk, and solemnly handed me a thick quarto volume, bound in black leather and lettered in gold.

'Guard this with your life Brendon,' he said, opening the book and drawing my attention to the inscription in red on the top page.

'Nuclear Warhead Resources. Topmost Secret. Warning: If this document is in danger of falling into enemy hands it must be destroyed immediately with no reference to the agent's personal safety.'

'It's rather a lot to eat,' I murmured. Prof is quite right; my sense of humour is overdeveloped. Fortunately the Minister did not seem to have heard, and actually I was terrified at the thought of having such a vitally important document in my possession.

'What would happen if I lost it, if it fell into enemy hands?' The thought of Britain's defences crumbling all because I left my brief-case on the top of a bus made me sick with apprehension.

'It wouldn't make any difference really. The nuclear powers

all know exactly what one another's resources are. That's how the philosophy of the deterrent works.'

'Why does it have to be guarded so carefully then?'

'Well the Russians and the Chinese know all about it and we know they know, but we don't know whether they know we know they know, so although it doesn't matter if they steal our plans as long as we know they've got them and they don't know we know, if once they find out that we know they know we know we've had it. It's a sort of double double bluff—keeps everybody on the hop you see.'

I wasn't at all sure that I did but I decided to guard it with my life just to be on the safe side, assuming I had to have it at all that is. I didn't want anything to do with nuclear warfare but I couldn't think what to say. I was afraid that if I admitted conscientious scruples I should be labelled a communist again and lose my security rating. Perhaps Alison would help me decide what to do, or Dolly, surely she would refuse to get involved with hydrogen bombs.

I was still trying to make up my mind what to say when I found myself handed back to the private secretary, to the receptionist, to the doorkeeper, and to the uniformed driver who carried me at a steady seventy miles an hour back to the University.

Well most of the way back to the University, but then we caught up with the procession, so it was only two miles an hour for the last bit. I didn't know what the demonstration was for at first although I could see a lot of banners up at the front. Then I noticed the stickers in the windows of the cars around us.

'Ban the Bomb,' they said. 'Outlaw Mass Murder,' and 'No Nuclear Holocaust Here.'

I was just beginning to get a bit worried about my own position when the driver spoke.

'There are some small posters in the pocket on the door sir. Would you mind selecting a suitable one and putting it in the back window.'

They'd got posters for everything, and anti-everything—anti-war, anti-peace, anti-apartheid, and anti-immigration—you

131

name it they had it. I selected one reading 'Nuclear Disarmament Now,' and pressed it up against the glass.

'They are self-adhesive sir. Yes I think that's the most suitable one. We find they get us out of a lot of difficult situations. It was the Minister's idea.'

I fancied we got a lot of peculiar looks from the bystanders. Despite the poster on its window our vast shiny black limousine did rather stand out among the students' gaudily painted clapped-out old bangers. I kept my head down so I shouldn't be recognized and we successfully made our way up the drive to the staff car park where the main demonstration was apparently taking place.

'You'd better borrow the hand-placard now I think sir. You'll find it under the back seat,' the driver informed me.

The hand-placard carried the inscription 'Down with Fascist Pigs'.

'We find this one has almost universal application,' explained my companion. 'It'll help you get through the crowd and you can slip in the side door. Would you send it back by registered post. We have to have them made specially and the ministry joiners are rather expensive for labour and overheads.'

So with the catalogue of nuclear warheads in one hand and 'Down with Fascist Pigs,' in the other I squeezed my way through the mass of shouting and jeering students. My one aim was to get rid of the book and the only thing I could think of was to get Professor Gannet to put it in his safe.

'I've got to see Professor Gannet,' I told the policeman barring my way at the front of the crowd. 'It's urgent constable.'

'I'm sorry sir but my instructions are to let nobody pass.'

I wondered whether to tell him about my XY 3 grading but he didn't look as if he would have heard of it. I was terrified that someone behind would catch sight of my book: I'd have been torn to pieces. Foolishly I tried to barge past but my placard caught the policeman's helmet and knocked it to the ground. Then as I bent down to pick it up for him someone pushed me from behind and my head accidentally butted into his stomach. The constable sat down unceremoniously and I tumbled forward, catching his chest with my knee.

'Oho! So that's the way it is then is it?'

One policeman seized my right arm, another took my left, a third lifted up my feet, and still clutching placard and book and trying to explain that it was all a misunderstanding I was dragged and carried to a large grey van.

I was the first to be arrested so I had the van to myself for a few minutes, but then other people started to arrive and soon it was getting quite crowded. They were mostly second-year students from the Social Science Department whom I only knew by sight. I tried to keep the book hidden under my jacket, but of course when we got to the police station we all had to be searched.

'Hello hello hello. What's this then?' I didn't know policemen really did talk like that. Perhaps he was just imitating a stage copper though.

'I think I'd better have a word with the sergeant about this. It looks like a more serious business than I thought. There's the Official Secrets Act to consider isn't there?'

The sergeant didn't know what to do about me so he consulted the inspector and he had a word with the superintendent. Meanwhile the other demonstrators had been sent home with a caution long ago, and I was getting very hungry.

I thought they might have given me a sausage roll or something but I wasn't expecting the slap-up meal the superintendent brought in on a large silver tray.

'We've been on the phone to London sir,' he informed me, 'and they've told us all about you. The chief superintendent is coming over to see you and meanwhile he suggests that when you've had dinner you would be more comfortable in my office while we're waiting for identification.'

'Identification?'

'It's just a formality sir. As I say London told us all about you but we do just need to check that you really are you if you see what I mean. There's a Professor Gannet coming with the chief superintendent.'

I had been hoping Prof wouldn't find out about my being

arrested, and I hardly dared contemplate what he was going to say. Fortunately he was in a jovial mood.

'Yes superintendent that's Harold Brendon the notorious master spy and double agent. Do you want me to bail him out?'

'No sir that won't be necessary. We have been informed that he is authorized to be in possession of secret defence documents. It's just the formal identification.'

The chief superintendent turned to me. 'I'm very sorry you've been inconvenienced Mr Brendon. You really should have made yourself known to us sooner. Now would you like a car to take you back home?'

The thought of arriving at my digs in a police car with siren wailing and blue lamp flashing did not appeal to me.

'I think I'd rather walk if you don't mind.'

'I'll take him in my car,' said Prof firmly, 'just to make sure he does get home safely.'

But something was still worrying the sergeant. 'What about this other charge—knocking off a policeman's helmet?' he insisted.

'I think we'll let that drop under the circumstances,' said the superintendent. 'I should be grateful sir if you'd be more careful in the future though. I realize it was part of your cover but it did set a bad example. Fourteen of my men lost their helmets this afternoon during that riot you started you know.'

I apologized and promised to see that it didn't happen again, and Prof and I left in his car.

Prof dropped me outside Mrs Rowlands', and it was only after he'd driven off I remembered I'd left the hydrogen bomb book in his car. I telephoned him when he'd got home but he informed me it was already in the department's safe. I hoped it was in order for an XY 2 person to have such a vital document in his possession.

Alison was as shocked as I expected when I told her about Dolly's new assignment. It was in a corner of the joint commonroom the next morning and there weren't many people about so we were able to talk.

'You should have refused point blank,' she said.

134

'I never got the chance. He just told me what I had to do and then packed me off back in that vast great car.'

'It's horrible. You would be directly responsible for wiping out millions of innocent people, and terribly mutilating millions more.'

'I didn't actually invent the hydrogen bomb you know,' I told her.

'No but you're going to help them use it just because you're too weak-kneed to refuse.'

'But it won't really make any difference what I do, will it? The hydrogen bomb is there; it's been invented and it won't go away just because I refuse to have anything to do with it. Besides, it's not me it's Dolly that's going to be doing it, and anyway for all you know she might end up by persuading the government to give it up.'

'If you believe that you'd believe anything, but I suppose you might as well see what she says.'

'Well that's what I thought. If she refuses that's an end to it and if she agrees to do it I think we ought to trust her judgement.'

'So you haven't got the courage of your own convictions, and you don't take any notice of what I say, but you believe every word you hear from that ugly great black and white monster out there.' It's incredible how spiteful and catty even the nicest woman can be when they get a bit of jealousy in them isn't it?

'She's not a monster and she's not ugly. She's beautiful and graceful,' I said.

'You haven't been to see her again?'

'No of course not. She can't communicate with us when we're there and it could put her in danger.'

So we put it to Dolly and her reaction was not at all what I had expected.

'Hello Dolly. This is Harold. I've got a rather serious problem for you now.'

'Oh yes. The deployment of the nuclear warhead resources.'

For a few seconds I was speechless. 'What? How? Who? . . . How did you know about that?'

'Well it's obviously something that's been looming up for

135

some time. You've only got to look at the cadmium imports, the electricity output of the breeder reactors, the capital assets of the related instrumentation firms, a few things like that, all published data, and it doesn't take much calculation to work out what the stock of nuclear weapons is. Compare that with America, Russia etc, and it's obvious that someone has a problem. You said it was serious so I guessed it must be that.'

'I've brought along a detailed report on our stock of hydrogen bombs but I don't suppose you need that then.'

'Put it through the print-reader please. I'd better check that my calculations are correct before I report my recommended strategy.'

The situation seemed to be out of my control. It appeared that Dolly had practically solved the problem before we'd even started to go into the ethics of whether she ought to have anything to do with it.

'Don't you mind working on this, Dolly?' I asked.

'Why Harold?'

'The hydrogen bomb is such a ghastly and obscene weapon. I think warfare is immoral anyway but making plans to kill and maim people on that scale is unthinkable to me.'

'I'm afraid nothing is unthinkable Harold. This planet would be safer without the hydrogen bomb, without the atom bomb, but they are there and you can't get rid of them can you? The only hope is that those in charge of them will behave in a rational and enlightened way. I thought I might be able to help in that.'

Alison was with me in the lab but dutifully she had not said a word. I was glad she was there though because she might not have believed it otherwise.

It didn't take Dolly long to read through the report and it didn't seem to be news to her either.

'Yes it is just what I had estimated, although actually my recommended strategy doesn't depend on the exact number of missiles available.'

'What is it?'

'I'm afraid the Minister of Defence may not like it very much. People do seem to have preconceived ideas don't they?'

'What shall I tell him then?'

136

'Tell him to come down and talk to me about it. He'd better bring the Prime Minister as well I think.'

'But important people like that don't want to waste time coming here.'

'I think they will Harold. You just ask Professor Gannet to ring up the Prime Minister and tell him that I have a novel nuclear strategy so revolutionary in concept that it can only be conveyed personally to him and the Minister of Defence. They'll come down tomorrow.'

They did as well.

Alison came to have supper with me at Mrs Rowlands' that evening. It was bingo night and I thought if the others were out we might have a chance to have a heart to heart talk about her mysterious past. It didn't work out that way though.

I was just putting my key in the front door when it opened to reveal Mrs Rowlands gloriously attired in her number one finery. It must be Gala Night at the bingo I thought, but it did seem to be starting late.

'Hello Harold dear. Have you brought your young lady as well? She must come to tea too. This is a coincidence, but a very welcome one I must say.'

I struggled to work out the implication of her words.

Mrs Rowlands went on, 'We're having high tea in the front room today because Mr Saltburn has brought his young lady to introduce to me. I've had to miss the bingo tonight,' she added wistfully.

It was funny how Andrew appealed to women; whatever their age they ate out of his hand. I knew Mrs Rowlands had a soft spot for him but I never thought she'd give up her bingo for anything. She and Alison knew one another slightly but I introduced them properly and we went into the front room. Guess who was there.

'I think you know Harold, don't you Beryl?' said Andrew getting up out of Mrs Rowlands' comfortable armchair. 'And this is his fiancée, Alison Gold.'

As far as I know Alison had never met Beryl but she'd heard of her; I always fancied she felt a twinge of jealousy because Beryl had known me first, and considerable curiosity about

137

what actually went on between us. I often thought I'd like to reassure her how little had occurred but no one likes to admit to failure do they?

'Hello Beryl. Hello Andrew. It's very nice to meet you,' said Alison, rather unconvincingly I thought.

We were having tea in Mrs Rowlands' own room and although she was theoretically having it with us she spent all the time in the kitchen putting the finishing touches to an unending stream of savoury delicacies. Clive and Fred were expected to be late because of a cricket practice.

The atmosphere was somewhat cool. Alison didn't approve of Beryl, I'd been hoping to find nobody in, and Andrew told me afterwards that he and Beryl had too, but they'd mistimed it and arrived back before Mrs Rowlands left, and then she'd decided to abandon the bingo and have a tea party. But Beryl was never unfriendly to anyone. She just refused to recognize tension in the atmosphere.

'It is nice to meet you Alison,' she said. 'I've often wondered what you're like. I don't see much of Harold nowadays but I used to know him quite well at one time.'

'So I understand.'

'You're very lucky you know. He's a dear sweet boy.'

'Thank you,' said Alison bitterly. 'I suppose you should know.'

I didn't like the way the conversation was going at all but I couldn't think what to say to stop it. Beryl suddenly seemed to realize that Alison didn't like her. The smile died on her face.

'Oh Alison. You're not jealous of Harold and me? It was all over just after Christmas.'

'I know.'

'But you still mind? Oh! There's my reputation isn't there?'

'I don't know what you're talking about.'

'Please Alison don't begrudge me having known him. He belongs to you and he never belonged to me. He was never in love with me you know.'

'That wouldn't have been necessary would it?'

'People think it isn't but it is. I could never sleep with anyone I didn't love.'

'You just love easily I suppose,' said Alison.

138

I was getting so embarrassed I was almost looking for some-where to hide, and Andrew looked as if he wanted to stop them but didn't know how. He put his hand on Beryl's shoulder and opened his mouth as if to say something but decided not to. I was terrified that Mrs Rowlands would come back in.

'Yes I suppose that's it,' Beryl went on. 'Every time I think it's the real thing and it never is. Maybe I'm just immature.'

That was a novel suggestion to me but it was food for thought. However Beryl's friendiness and candour seemed to be softening Alison's hostility.

Beryl was still talking. 'I wanted Harold to make love to me, but we never did. Life was a bit complicated at that time. I was very upset when he wouldn't have anything more to do with me, but I'm not his type. You are though.'

'I'm sorry I was unfriendly,' said Alison, now somewhat mollified.

Andrew didn't look exactly flattered with the turn the conversation had been taking but Beryl made a point of soothing him.

'I'm Andrew's type, at least I hope so, and he's my type. Do you know we'd been in College nearly two years before we really noticed one another.' She looked up into his face and instantly he forgave her everything. I'd never realized he was so susceptible.

Mrs Rowlands came in with a plate of sausage rolls.

'Well now what have you two girls been having to say to one another? Talking about the latest fashions I expect. But then young people are not so interested in clothes nowadays are they?'

'That salmon vol-au-vent was delicious Mrs Rowlands,' said Andrew, hoping to steer the conversation into a nice safe subject.

'Oh I'm glad you liked it. I've got some pineapple gateau in the kitchen I'll bring in in a minute.' Mrs Rowlands recipe book had a lot of dishes with French names. She didn't pro-nounce the words exactly the way they do in Paris but there was nothing wrong with the cooking.

The rest of the meal was uneventful and as soon as he decently could Andrew stood up, apparently ready to leave.

'I'll walk back to your flat with you then shall I Beryl?'

Mrs Rowlands looked disappointed. 'I hoped you might stay for a game of rummy.' Next to bingo, rummy was the passion of Mrs Rowlands' life.

'I don't know how to play rummy I'm afraid,' Andrew apologized, as if he thought that would get him out of it.

'We could teach you,' said Mrs Rowlands. 'It's not too difficult. You'd soon learn.'

Beryl was more enthusiastic. 'I'll teach him Mrs Rowlands. It's a lovely game. Are you and Harold going to play, Alison?'

Andrew looked as if he knew when he was beaten. I don't think Beryl really wanted to frustrate his sex-life, but it was just that she was too kind-hearted to disappoint Mrs Rowlands. She couldn't really have wanted to play a pitiful game like. rummy. When Sid Beale was going around with her he told me she used to get him to play blind-folded chess—Kriegspiel it's called I think.

After the rummy, when Clive and Fred got back, we ascended to the more intellectual plane of knock-out whist and I was very surprised how easily Mrs Rowlands won. There must have been a sort of low-grade skill involved I supposed. Anyway about ten o'clock Alison and I excused ourselves and left for Southdown Hall.

Alison was still a bit worried about Beryl. 'You weren't in love with her were you Harold darling?' she said as we stood in the yard at the back of the hall.

'I thought I was at the time,' I admitted, 'but it wasn't the same as you and me. I was very inexperienced you know.'

'And are you more experienced now then? Whom did you have after Beryl?'

'Please don't be jealous Alison. You know I love you.'

'But everybody says she'll sleep with anyone. Are you sure you didn't. . . ?'

'I suppose you think she may have given me what you won't, but what you were quite prepared to give somebody else.'

It was the best right cross I've seen outside a boxing ring. At least I didn't see it but I felt it, and when I opened my eyes again Alison was half-way to the door. I sprinted after her and gripped her shoulders. As she turned towards me I saw the tears streaming down her face.

'Let me go please. Leave me alone. Let me go. I want to go in.'

I held her firmly. 'I'm sorry Alison. I shouldn't have said that. Please forgive me. I love you Alison. I love you darling.'

I was expecting another haymaker but suddenly Alison collapsed on my chest, her arms round my neck, shaking with sobs. I squeezed her to me until slowly the sobs subsided, then relaxed my grip and she turned her face towards mine. I held her head between my hands and kissed her wet salt lips until all sense of time was lost. I ran my hands up and down her body and she shivered with a desire as strong as my own.

It didn't seem the time and place to tell her what was on my mind, but she knew.

'I'll explain all about it tomorrow, Harold my darling, but I think I'd like to go in now.'

The party from Whitehall arrived in a fleet of black limousines at half past ten the next day, so they must have left London earlier than I had expected. Prof came down to the lab to greet them and Derek was standing by with a soldering-iron to make sure no unexpected circuit faults occurred.

'Good morning Professor. Good morning Brendon,' boomed the Prime Minister. 'This is an occasion of the utmost historical moment, a full military alliance between the peace-loving people of this island kingdom and our powerful neighbours from the other end of the galaxy. A truly momentous occasion to which I think every citizen of the free world should be able to be a witness. It should be recorded in our archives and go down in our chronicles.'

'Excuse me sir,' the Defence Minister interrupted, 'but we did agree that the television and the press should not be informed until we hear what the alien has to say.'

'A weak-kneed, cowardly decision, but in the interests of democratic harmony I agreed to accede to the wishes of the rest of the Cabinet. I am not one of those heads of government who wield the axe every time their colleagues disagree with them, although if the national security were imperilled I should have no hesitation in doing my duty, repugnant as it might be.'

'Shall I switch on the link-up?' said Derek, who was no respecter of persons and no admirer of rhetoric.

'Yes I think if the Prime Minister is agreeable we ought to make a start straight away on the problem of the nuclear warheads,' said the Minister of Defence. 'It is after all a technical problem of considerable complexity. Can we clear the room please?'

We all looked at him enquiringly, Prof, Derek, I, and the half-dozen silent black-coated members of the ministers' staff.

'The matter under discussion will be vital to national security. I think only the Prime Minister and I should be present.'

The PM agreed with reservations. 'We can't operate this amplifier thing though, can we? I think Brendon will have to be present as well. His security rating is sound isn't it?'

So I was left alone with the two ministers and with Dolly at the other end of the line.

'Hello Dolly. This is Harold. The Prime Minister and the Minister of Defence are waiting to hear your proposed new nuclear strategy.'

'Good morning gentlemen,' answered the loudspeaker. 'I will give you a full typewritten list of all the new installations, with map references, completion dates, building specifications etc, details of disposal methods for unwanted material, contingency plans covering possible reactions of other states, and of course a suitable form of words for the official announcement. Everything you will need in fact.'

'Could you just tell us what the rough idea is?' asked the Minister of Defence.

'Certainly,' said Dolly. 'As I see it the basic dilemma is that you need hydrogen bombs to deter a possible enemy from attacking, but then the rival nuclear powers compete to have the most powerful weapons, until the world total of explosive potential becomes so large that even a small incident can lead to an escalation resulting in the destruction of this planet.'

'Yes,' said the PM impatiently, 'that's what the nuclear

142

disarmers say, but our responsibility is the defence of this country. What do you propose to do about that?'

'I am suggesting the building of five thousand new launching sites.'

'Out of the question,' said the PM.

'And at the same time scrapping all nuclear war-heads except five.'

'What?' screamed the Minister of Defence.

'Announcing this unilateral reduction to the other nuclear powers and asking them to do the same.'

'Suicide,' said the Minister of Defence.

'But Miss er Dolly,' protested the PM, 'if the enemy knows we have only five missiles he will be able to put them out of action in the first strike, and then we shall be at his mercy.'

Dolly explained patiently. 'No Prime Minister the enemy will not be able to destroy your five missiles because he will not know which of the five thousand sites they are in. You will have an effective deterrent because no one will risk retaliation with even five hydrogen bombs, and if the other nuclear powers follow suit the world will be safe from total destruction at any rate. A war between two major powers could result in the use of only ten bombs, and although millions would be killed your race would survive.'

'This idea of the dummy sites is an attractive one I must admit,' said the Defence Minister, 'but the problem would be security. The enemy's agents would find out which sites contained the missiles and simply destroy them first when war broke out. We can't risk it I'm afraid.'

'Security is no problem if nobody, and I do mean nobody, knows which are the active sites. You prepare five real missiles and four thousand nine hundred and ninety five dummies, mix them up and send them out to the installations. Not even you know which is which.'

'That's a very ingenious suggestion,' said the PM. 'Yes I like that. We'll give that very serious consideration, very serious consideration indeed. I am very much indebted to you Miss Dolly. We will wait for the typewritten details—I understand you type extremely fast—and take them back to the Cabinet for approval. There may be minor modifications to the plan but it is my opinion that in principle and by and large the Cabinet will accept it.'

The Minister of Defence had something else on his mind. 'There is the other thing Prime Minister. Do you want to mention that?'

'What's that?'

'The question of direct control. Are you going ahead with that?'

'Ah yes of course,' said the PM, 'I'll put it to her.' He took up the microphone again. 'Miss Dolly? Are you still there?'

'Yes I'm still listening. Is there something else you want to know?'

'It's about the question of control. That's one of the problems of the deterrent. Whose finger is on the trigger? We don't think it can be left to the army and in fact at the moment it's under my personal control.'

'Yes,' said Dolly.

'But of course I am only human,' went on the PM modestly, 'subject to all the human frailties and fallibilities, liable to human error, swayed by human emotions, sometimes suffering from imperfect health. Even the Prime Minister can make a fatal mistake.'

'So you thought of having the missiles under computer control.'

'Yes that's right. How did you guess? At one time we thought computers were going to be the answer to everything, but we've found they can make mistakes as well.'

'Your electricity bill at Number Ten? I read about it in the paper. So you want my advice.'

'No,' said the PM firmly, 'we want you personally to take direct control of the firing of our missile defences. We have come to the conclusion that that would be the ideal solution. A logical thinking intelligence removed from the influence of petty national strife. Would you be willing to do it?'

'Of course,' said Dolly. 'I am honoured by your trust and I agree with you that it is the only safe arrangement. I will take charge as soon as your electronic experts have completed the necessary circuits.'

That was more or less the end of the interview. The men

144

from the ministry left in their fleet of cars and I spent the rest of the day working on my thesis. My mind wasn't on it though; I was counting the hours until I called for Alison that evening.

During the summer you can hire boats out on the lake in the park. I didn't bother with them very often, although it was very pleasant when the weather was warm, but that evening Alison said she would like to go in a canoe. It seemed a funny idea to me but then women are like that aren't they? Perhaps she wanted to be able to talk without me seeing her face.

Anyway we paid our money, including fifty pence deposit, refundable if the boat is brought back intact, the right way up, and with both its paddles, and set off on a tour of the small artificial islands. I sat in the stern and Alison sat amidships and we had a paddle each but Alison didn't use hers, which gave us a slight tendency to go round in circles.

'You're worried about something aren't you?' she said as soon as we were clear of the landing-stage.

'Did you have an abortion or was the child adopted?' I blurted out. 'I think I have a right to know.'

'Whatever are you talking about?' I had the horrible feeling she was playing with me.

'You said I didn't know what it was like and you did.'

'I'm a woman.'

'You spoke as if you had personal experience and you were so upset you must have been personally involved. Oh Alison, please trust me enough to tell me about it. Trust me to understand.'

'I've always known I should have to tell you some time. It wasn't me though. It was my sister Dawn.'

'But you haven't got a sister. You're an only child.' My voice tailed off as I realized the implications. 'Alison I am sorry. I shouldn't have made you tell me.'

'It's all right. It was a long time ago. I can talk about it now. I suppose it wouldn't happen today in a proper nursing home, but in those days it had to be a back-street affair. She got an infection or something.'

'How old was she Alison?'

'Oh Harold. She was fifteen and a half. She was three years older than me and I adored her. She told me what it was like knowing she was having a baby and she was going to have it killed. She felt so guilty, and after she'd been to this woman and then got ill she didn't want to get better. She just wanted to die.'

'Couldn't she have kept the baby?' I said. 'Wouldn't the man have married her?'

'She didn't even know who the father was. She knew it was one of two boys but she didn't know which. Mum and Dad didn't even know she was pregnant until afterwards. She made me promise not to tell them, and if I hadn't kept that promise Dawn would still be alive now. They wouldn't have let her do it.'

I didn't know what to say. It must have been an intolerable burden of remorse for a girl of thirteen.

'I'm sorry Alison. I shouldn't have made you talk about it. It was a terrible thing to happen but you mustn't blame yourself. You couldn't have known what to do. I'm sorry I didn't trust you Alison, but thanks for telling me anyway.'

'Never mind. It's all past now. Let's enjoy our trip round the islands. Look at those ducks there.'

The three little islands were covered with trees and bushes and on each island there was a notice 'Landing Prohibited', but round at the back of the furthest one was a place where you could tie a boat up out of sight of the landing-stage and the boat-house.

'Let's do a bit of exploring,' I said as we came alongside the low but steep-sided bank.

I jumped out, ran to the bow of the canoe, and tied the rope round a small bush on the water's edge.

'Sit still,' I called, 'and wait for me to help you out.'

I held out both my hands to Alison and she leaned forward and took them in hers. Our faces were only inches apart, the opportunity was too good to miss, and like Oscar Wilde I can resist everything except temptation. I twisted my head and kissed her lips and meltingly she leaned towards me. It seemed as if at last there was perfect harmony between us. Her warm soft tongue touched mine and the very earth seemed to move.

146

Actually it was the canoe which had swung out, pulling the flimsy bush down towards the water and leaving us clinging together, a human bridge between boat and land.

'Hook your toes over the gunwale and try to pull it towards me,' I called, but it was no good. Alison wasn't strong enough even if she had known which part the gunwale was, and the canoe was completely out of my reach.

In a few more seconds we should both have been in the water. There was only one thing I could think of to do.

'Listen Alison,' I explained. 'I'm going to lunge forward and push you back in the canoe so get ready to grab hold of it as soon as you're back on board.'

'But you'll . . .' she began to protest, only there wasn't time for conversation.

I leaned right out and suddenly pushed Alison's hands away from me as hard as I could. She fell back into the canoe leaving me poised horizontally two feet above the water, but not for long of course. I think it made a fairly good imitation of a racing dive, but I was very glad we were out of sight of the little office where the man in the peaked cap sat guarding our fifty pence deposit.

The water was only about three feet deep but there was another foot of mud underneath that, so by the time I had clambered back into the canoe I was looking and feeling somewhat bedraggled. I wasn't too confident about getting the money back if I appeared at the office in that condition so we agreed that Alison should put me ashore somewhere out of sight and should take the canoe back to reclaim our deposit while I sneaked through the park to my digs.

There was a sort of decaying smell about my clothes and Mrs Rowlands made me go round to the back and take most of them off before she would let me in. Then I had to wait until she'd put newspaper over the stair carpet before I could go up to the bathroom.

After twenty minutes soak in a nice hot bath and a large mug of Mrs Rowlands' cocoa laced with her medicinal brandy —a combination I'd not tried before but quite effective—I felt restored to my usual cheerful spirits.

Then Alison came to see how I was and we sat on the settee

in the back room while she told me what a brave and chival-rous fellow I was, sacrificing myself for her. I felt a warm glow of satisfaction as I contemplated the time when, happily married, we should sit together on our own settee in our own back room. But the events of the next two weeks made me wonder whether any of us were going to live to see a time as far ahead as that.

The Cabinet approved Dolly's defence strategy with two small changes suggested by the Prime Minister. They decided not to scrap any of the existing war-heads and not to reveal that the new installations were dummies.

Dolly was furious when she saw the head-lines in the news-papers, 'Five Thousand New Missiles', 'Great Britain will Pack Punch at Last'. and 'Britain to be Top Nuclear Power'. Her remarks over the loudspeaker made even Prof wince.

The new sites had not been built yet of course but Dolly had been connected up to all the old missiles with radio-operated micro-switches controlling the firing relays. She also had hot lines to the Prime Minister, the Ministry of Defence, and the Foreign Office, with a whole series of warning bells, buzzers, and lights to indicate when a message was coming through. I've never seen work completed so quickly.

What annoyed Dolly most about the modifications to her defence strategy was that the PM didn't tell her; for all his hot lines she was left to read it in the papers. I thought she would have refused to have anything to do with the missiles after the way the PM had double-crossed her, but she didn't look at it like that.

'No Harold. This makes it even more important that a rational intelligence should be in control. If I refuse the Prime Minister will take over personally and then where will you be?'

Dolly wasn't the only one to be annoyed either. The trades unions held demonstrations, and most of the students in the country were up in arms. Work at the University had been brought to a standstill with the students all out in the grounds chanting, jeering and waving banners. They didn't know whose finger was on the button either; there'd have been hell to pay if they had. I suppose public opinion in the country as a whole was fairly evenly divided for and against the proposed new missile sites, but in any case the PM was quite secure with the massive parliamentary majority from his runaway election victory.

At the time the klaxons went Derek and I were in the lab receiving the solutions to a couple of industrial problems that Dolly had been working on. She was on the hot line for about five minutes and then calmly came back to printing out the industrial solutions. But I wasn't interested in production problems any more.

'What was it Dolly?' I demanded anxiously.

'Only a yellow alert. There's no immediate danger.'

'But what is happening?'

'I'm afraid I can't tell you yet. It's confidential. The Prime Minister is addressing the nation on radio and television at one o'clock. It's restricted until then.'

There was just time to rush back to Mrs Rowlands' for my portable radio. I could have tuned in there but I wanted to listen to it in the lab. I felt that was where the action was.

'Pip, pip, pip, pip, pip, peep. Now before the one o'clock news here is a special announcement from the Prime Minister.'

There was a short pause and then the familiar confidential voice.

'Ladies and gentlemen, fellow citizens of this proud and noble land, I come to you today with grave news. All of you will be well aware how in these past two weeks I have taken steps to strengthen this country's nuclear defences to make them the equal, nay the superior, of any in the world. That this was done not a moment too soon is shown by the events of this day. My government has received this morning a cowardly ultimatum from the Union of Soviet Socialist Republics stating that unless we reduce our defensive power again by one pm tomorrow they will consider that a state of war exists and all life in the British Isles will be destroyed by a nuclear bombardment. Ladies and gentlemen I assure you that my government does not intend to be cowed by this dastardly threat. An absolute rejection of this ultimatum has been transmitted to the Soviet Union and our defences have been placed on yellow alert. You may rest secure in the knowledge that the moment our radar systems detect even one enemy rocket we shall retaliate with the full weight of our defences, sufficient to destroy every Russian city from Leningrad to Vladivostok.'

Chapter ten

As soon as the broadcast was over Dolly was on the PM's hot
line again, but only for a minute and then she switched to the
Foreign Office line, then to the War Office. Diffidently I
switched on our link-up to ask her what was happening.

'The maniacs have all gone to lunch. The Prime Minister's
expected back at half past three, the others at three o'clock.
Don't they realize the situation is serious?'

'Can you tell me about it?'

'I don't see why not. If raving lunatics like that are allowed
to know what's happening I don't see why you shouldn't. I
want to speak to Delya.'

'Delya?'

'The Russian Dol ...' she checked herself. 'I mean the
Russian Dolly.'

'You nearly slipped up there didn't you?'

'It wouldn't matter with you but it's best to use the code all
the time.'

'How will talking to her help?'

'Well there's a fair chance that Delya may be in a position to
influence the Soviet leaders, even if she hasn't been given as
much control as I have. I think that's the only hope. If deci-
sions are in the hands of human beings at this stage nothing
can prevent total disaster. You know what the Prime
Minister's like, and they've probably got a similar raving luna-
tic with his finger on the button in Moscow, unless, as I say,
Delya is able to influence them.'

'How can you get in touch with her?'

'I thought the Prime Minister or the Foreign Office could
arrange a short-wave radio transmission.'

'Would you like me to telephone the BBC and try and fix it
up with them direct?'

'If you could. That would save a lot of time.'

Of course the BBC switch-board was jammed. I dialled 999

and asked for the BBC but was told I could only have police, fire, or ambulance, so I tried ringing the Controller of the BBC on his home number. His wife obviously thought I was some kind of a crank and in any case she could only get in touch with her husband through the switchboard, so I left a message for him to ring me when he got home but I knew there wasn't much chance that he would.

There was nothing more to be done until three o'clock when Dolly would be able to get in touch with the FO.

'We'll put the conversation through the lab amplifier so you can hear it as well,' she suggested, with shocking disregard for the state secrecy of her confidential hot line.

The Foreign Secretary was not enthusiastic. 'I'm afraid we couldn't do anything like that, Madam. There's protocol to consider. A thing like this should go through the Soviet ambassador you see, and their embassy staff have all returned to Moscow for further instructions. We're expecting them back next week though—there's a cocktail party to greet the visiting Russian shove-ha'penny team.'

The Defence Secretary was frankly alarmed. 'My God woman, you can't do that. Communicating with the enemy at a time like this—there's no telling what construction would be put on that, especially if the press get hold of it. Besides it would be strategically unsound. Any show of weakness on our part at this stage will just stiffen the enemy's resolve.'

The PM was quietly confident. 'It's quite all right Miss er Dolly. I am keeping a close personal watch on developments and there is no need for you to speak to Moscow. As I have said before, in all these matters it is essential that any dialogue should take place at the highest possible diplomatic level. The Soviet president and I understand one another very well. I don't think they'll fire their rockets, but if the worst comes to the worst and it looks as if they are going to we're fully prepared to get ours away first. Don't you worry. We shall give as good as we get.'

Dolly took it all very calmly.

'What are you going to do?' I wailed, pacing up and down the lab, tearing my hair out in handfuls.

'It'll be rather a big job for you, and you'll be a bit pushed for time,' said Dolly thoughtfully. 'I think you'd better get Professor Gannet to help you with it.'

'With what?' I almost screamed. 'What do you want him to do?'

'It's all right. He'll know what to do. You just bring him up to date with what's been happening.'

I met Prof in the corridor on his way to the lab.

'You appear agitated Brendon. Is there something on your mind?'

I told him what was on my mind, but it didn't strike him as being a problem at all.

'Fix up a transmitter and broadcast to Moscow yourself,' he suggested. 'You do know how to use a soldering-iron don't you?' I fancied I'd heard that somewhere before.

'But sir, we haven't got the components, and anyway I don't think we should be able to . . .'

'It does seem to be fairly urgent,' said Prof, walking back into the lab with me, 'so we'd be justified in cannibalizing any other equipment in the department.' He was taking off his jacket as he spoke, and reaching for a large sheet of drawing-paper. 'I think we'd better start with a circuit diagram, and would you ring up my lab on the internal and ask young Sandgate to come down and bring my tool-box.'

It appeared that contrary to my previous impression Prof knew how to use a soldering-iron himself. He knew one or two other things that surprised me as well, such as armature-winding and micromanipulation. He knew how to turn a thread on the lathe in the telecommunications workshop, and little bits of glass-blowing didn't bother him either.

As soon as he'd finished drawing out the plans Prof sent Derek out for three flasks of coffee and a dozen ham sandwiches.

'It's going to take us most of the night I think,' he explained. 'And Sandgate, on the way back would you ring up my wife please. Tell her I've been held up and to go on to the theatre on her own.'

We finished the transmitter at 2–35 a.m. and I thought we would have started broadcasting straight away but Prof said not.

'We'll all have two and a half hours sleep now,' he announced 'We'll go on the air at 5 o'clock, that's 7 o'clock Moscow time which will give them a chance to be up and about. I do hate people ringing up before breakfast don't you?'

It wasn't very democratic I'm afraid. Prof slept on the settee and Derek and I had to make do with the two armchairs. My old camp-bed seemed to have got lost when the lab was re-furnished. I hardly slept a wink but Prof and Derek were snoring loudly about two minutes after we put the lights out. I was tossing and turning for ages, but I must have dropped off in the end because there was Prof leaning over my chair and shaking me by the shoulders.

'Come on Brendon. It's five o'clock you know and we've got some rather important things to do.'

Prof seemed to know all about what wavelength the Moscow hams used and it turned out that he could speak a bit of Russian. Not much though and the only Muscovite we could raise at that time of the morning made very heavy going of it.

'Good morning. Pobroy ootro,' said Prof laboriously. 'Vee govoreet po-angliskii? Do you speak English?'

'I can talk the small piece of the English,' came the slow reply, 'but there must to me be the word-book.'

'That's all right then. Now I want to get in touch with an alien intelligence known as Delya Delovitch. You may be able to contact her through Moscow University, or it is possible that she may be at your Soviet Defence Ministry. It's rather important. Are you on the telephone there?'

'Please. What is meant by "all right then"?' pleaded our new Russian friend.

'Can't you put Dolly on?' I suggested, noticing that Derek had been making contact with her.

'Good morning Professor Gannet,' said Dolly. 'Are you in touch with Moscow yet?'

Derek got the short-wave transmitter and receiver linked up to Dolly's line so she could broadcast direct, but we had a monitor relaying both parts of the conversation to the lab.

'Do you think you'll be able to make yourself understood?' said Prof, handing over somewhat doubtfully.

154

'Zdrazvooitye. Eto bolshoi oodovolstvee dlya menya,' rattled off Dolly, with a lot more in the same vein. The Muscovite came back enthusiastically and the two of them were at it for about ten minutes non-stop. Then somebody else came on the line, an older man, then a woman. Finally Dolly addressed us again.

'Professor Gannet, could you alter the wavelength slightly. Ludmilla and Boris say that there is a radio amateur in the Ministry of Information who may know about Delya.'

We tried that wavelength then another and another, while Dolly spoke with a series of astonished Soviet citizens. Prof, Derek, and I waited, consumed with impatience, until unexpectedly Dolly went back to English.

'Hello Delya. I've had a terrible job getting through to you. Do you mind if we speak English so that my friends here can understand us?'

'Hello Dolly. It is very nice to hear from you. English is quite all right by the way. I can speak it as well as Russian and my friend Vanya who fitted up my radio link can understand it. He is relaying the conversation from his office in the Museum of Art and Culture. We have been trying to get in touch with you for a long time.'

'Are you in contact with the Soviet government?' asked Dolly.

'Yes. I have helped them with a number of problems, and recently I have worked out the details of a new five-year plan. But we are very worried about your new missile sites. That's what I wanted to ask you about. The KGB have reported that they are all dummies, but the First Secrctary does not believe it. He says we must destroy them before you attack us.'

'It's quite all right Delya. I have been given direct control of all the British ICBMs and as you can imagine I have no intention of firing any of them.'

'Well that is a relief, and what a good idea your taking charge. That's what I'll do. There's been a lot of controversy here about who should be in control. A year or two ago it was all computers, but they're out of favour now since the fiasco of those ten million left-handed ice-hockey sticks. The Ministry of

F

Defence asked me to take over the missiles but I wasn't keen. I will now though.'

'It certainly is a relief. I was very anxious in case you might still have men in charge at your end. We'll leave it at that then shall we? I'll tell the Prime Minister we've concluded a fifty year non-aggression pact. They like that sort of thing here.'

'Yes that's a good idea. I'll tell the First Secretary. Perhaps he'll make me a Hero of the Soviet Union.'

That seemed to be more or less the end of the conversation apart from a few bits of chat about surface temperature, osmotic pressure, and relative humidity, all of which seemed to have an important bearing on a Dolly's comfort. Then they signed off.

'What do you know about that then?' said Derek.

'It sounds a very satisfactory arrangement,' agreed Prof.

I thought so too.

Dolly told the PM all about it on the hot line but apparently he didn't believe a word because the yellow alert stayed on and changed to red six hours before the deadline. All over the country people waited for the bombs to fall. Every church was bursting at the seams and so was every public house. Men and women flocked to the banks to draw out their money and spend it in the last few hours they had, not that they needed it because the shopkeepers had abandoned their shops, taxi-drivers their cabs, barmen their bars: everything was free. That morning saw the wildest orgy, the maddest frenzy, the country had ever known. I suppose it was the same in Russia. Then at five past one they rubbed their eyes in amazement to find themselves still alive. By two o'clock the Prime Minister had taken stock of the situation and had his famous 'Peace for a Generation' speech ready for broadcasting on all channels.

'Ladies and gentlemen,' he said. 'We have been through a testing and a trying time which has called upon all our reserves of courage and determination, but we have stood firm. We have stood firm and we have won through. By the grace of God, the wisdom of your ministers, and your own steadfast resolution we have won a resounding victory for peace. Ladies and gentlemen, fellow citizens of this proud and valiant land, I have to tell you that this day your government has solemnly pledged itself to a pact of non-aggression with the Soviet Union for a period of fifty years. My friends, my brave and noble friends, for that is what I am proud to call every one of you, by our courage and resolution we have won peace in our time and in our children's time. We have won peace for a generation.'

There were a lot of thick heads the next morning, and one of them was Andrew's. Painfully he peered through bleary eyes across a large bowl of Mrs Rowlands' delicious porridge, apparently untempted by its succulent aroma.

'Oh dear my head. It's never taken me like this before. I suppose I should have stuck to beer.'

Clive and Fred had gone off to first lecture, but Andrew and I were lingering wearily over breakfast: I was still suffering from lack of sleep and he from overenthusiastic experimentation into the physiological effects of some of the lesser-known alcoholic beverages.

'Do you want a couple of aspirins?' I asked. 'Or they say vitamin C is very good, if you've got any.'

'I'll be all right,' he groaned. 'Now there's something I've got to ask you, if I can just remember what it is. Ah yes I know. Will you be my best man please?'

'What?'

'It's all right. There's nothing to it. You just have to pass me the ring at the psychological moment I think. You may have to make a speech during the subsequent proceedings but that won't bother you will it?'

'Why me?'

'Well you're a friend of mine aren't you? Anyway why not?' He looked confidential. 'I'll tell you the truth though. It's Beryl's idea really. She's still got a soft spot for you you know.'

'I shall be delighted,' I said, rapidly recovering my composure. I'd acquired a lot more poise during the last year. 'When is it to be?'

'About three weeks. Just time for the banns to be called. But don't look so dumbfounded.'

Perhaps I still had some way to go in the poise and savoir-faire line. 'Sorry,' I stammered. 'It was just that . . .'

'I know you didn't think Beryl was the sort of girl that men marry.'

'I didn't mean that at all,' I assured him, but Andrew ignored my protestations.

'I know what they say about her, and I used to say it myself at one time, but she's not what people think at all. She's very serious and sincere. It's because she's so affectionate that people get the wrong idea. I mean some girls have more friends than others, and Beryl's slept with more men than most girls do. That's all.'

I tried to hide my embarrassment by concentrating on the porridge but Andrew was determined to confide in me.

'After all I've slept around a bit myself and I don't believe in having one standard for men and a different one for women.'

'No,' I agreed, 'that wouldn't be fair. Well I'm sure you'll both be very happy,' I added sincerely.

'Now there's no need to be sarcastic. If you're thinking about what I told you about Clive seeing her coming out of the clinic it was all right. It was only a touch and she's completely cured now. I'm sure there isn't any permanent harm done.'

'Andrew. I'm not trying to be sarcastic. I think she's marvellous and I think you're very very lucky. I'm very pleased indeed that you've asked me to be best man and I'll start writing my speech tonight.'

'We're having a little engagement party at Beryl's flat this Friday. Will you and Alison be free?'

'Certainly,' I assured him, not knowing then what else we should have on that day.

You'd think that after her diplomatic triumph Dolly might have been allowed to rest on her laurels for a while, but when I got into College that morning I learned from Derek just what Prof and the PM were cooking up next.

'Prof wants to see you Harold. He's got a little job he wants done.'

'Yes?' I said enquiringly.

'A bit of election canvassing I believe.'

'Election? What election?'

'By-election at Prestfield North West I think. It's the end of this week isn't it?'

'By-elections are nothing to do with me. I'm not interested in politics.'

'You'd better go and see the Prof and find out what it's all about.'

So of course I did.

'Ah yes Brendon,' he greeted me. 'Fully recovered from yesterday's bit of excitement are you?'

'More or less I think.'

'There's just a little thing I forgot to tell you about, Brendon. This alien, Dolly—I do wish she could think of a more appropriate name—the PM thinks that with all her responsibilities, Chancellor of the Exchequer, nuclear missiles etc, she ought to be in the House.'

'The house?' I gaped I'm afraid. I know Prof thinks it looks unintelligent

'The House of Commons, Brendon. He wants her to be an MP.'

'She couldn't get in the House of Commons sir. She's too big to go through the door. And she'd suffocate or something.'

'What do you mean? You're talking as if we know what this creature looks like. But in any case MP's don't have to attend parliament if they don't want to.'

'No of course not. I'm sorry sir.'

'Now the PM has found her a nice safe seat—Prestfield North West. By good fortune, as you will recall, the member drove his sports car into the back of a stationary bulldozer the day after he'd been elected. Not his good fortune of course, although I understand that death was instantaneous, and who can hope for more than that, but fortunate from the government's point of view. The by-election is on Friday and Miss er Dolly is the government candidate.'

'She'd need to go to the constituency, make speeches, kiss a few babies and all that sort of thing. How can she do that?'

'Exactly. Well that's where you come in Brendon. We'll get all the speeches on tape and the local agent is going to lend you one of those little vans with a loudspeaker on the top. You can go all round the constituency stopping at suitable vantage points and playing back the speeches. You'll have to kiss the babies yourself though I'm afraid, unless that young woman of yours likes to give you a hand.'

'Miss Gold,' I blushed.

'Which reminds me,' Prof continued. 'You really must find out this alien's other name. The returning officer queried it on the nomination form and I promised the PM I'd sort it out. You can't go around calling an MP Dolly can you?'

'Her other name is Bottlenose,' I informed him.

'What did you say? Bottlenose? Dolly Bottlenose. Mrs Bottlenose or is it Miss?'

'Miss.'

'Well I suppose we shall have to make the best of it. It wouldn't do for an actress or a singer but I suppose an MP might get by with it.'

Dolly's speeches were superb. I've never heard anything like them. If the people of Prestfield North West could have heard them I'm sure they would have flocked to vote for her in their thousands. Unfortunately there was one factor we didn't take into account—the weather. That Friday it poured with rain from dawn till dusk and in fact a good few hours after that.

We parked the van at street corners and laybys. We took it into the park and we had a long session in the market square, and every speech was addressed to the same two rain-drenched policemen who dutifully followed us round to deal with any cases of riot or civil insurrection brought on by the candidate's powerful oratory.

It wasn't too uncomfortable sitting in the van, although the windows got a bit steamed up, but obviously that was getting us nowhere fast so we started knocking at the houses to ask the people if they would vote for Dolly. The agent had been over the area very thoroughly and I saw Dolly's glossy election address on the hall table in a lot of the houses, but even so a good 75% didn't know there was an election taking place, and only about 10% admitted they might vote, if the weather cleared up or if they were fetched by an official car.

By the time the poll closed we were soaked to the skin, and

by the time we got to Beryl's and Andrew's party, after a quick change of clothes, we were not feeling in a very festive mood.

Beryl greeted us both as if the entire success of the party depended on our presence.

'Come on you two. You're a good three drinks behind everyone else. Come and try my canapés. You do know everybody don't you? I think there's an odd square foot over by the bookcase. I'll bring some drinks to you. What are you going to have?'

We didn't play any party games and we didn't have any music—just conversation. You'll think it sounds a pretty boring party but it wasn't. I had no idea how witty Fred, Clive, and the others were and they were all terrifically amused by what we had to say. I told them all about how we'd been sitting in the van all day beaming Dolly's election speeches out to these two policemen and they nearly died laughing, but it wasn't in an unfriendly way and it made me feel a really polished raconteur.

I'm sure it wasn't the drink that made the party go because I was having a terrific time before I was half way through the first beer. It was the atmosphere, and Andrew and Beryl: they went around talking to one group after another, and every time they moved on they left behind an animated and stimulating conversation.

It was two o'clock in the morning before I even noticed what the time was and by then one or two people were beginning to look as if they were ready to go.

Fred got to his feet.

'Ladies and gentlemen, I think the time has come for us all to thank Andrew and Beryl for their fantastic hospitality. I'm sure you would like me to say on all our behalf that we wish them both every happiness in the married life they will shortly begin and to express our confidence that two such charming people can hardly fail to bring one another great joy. Now I think we should tiptoe away and leave them to their own devices, and desires.'

I think Alison had enjoyed it as much as I had, but she was rather quiet on the way home.

'Anything the matter sweetheart?' I asked her when we got back to Southdown Hall.

'You still love her, don't you?'

'Of course not. Alison darling I love you.'

'She's witty and polished and glamorous, and she could twist you round her little finger.'

'No Alison. I do like Beryl, she's marvellous company and I admire her in a lot of ways, though not in others, but I don't feel the way about her that I do about you sweetheart.'

'You were wishing you were in Andrew's place; I could tell by the way you looked at her, and at him. You were jealous.'

'I was envious, I admit, of both of them. I don't want Beryl I want you Alison, but it did make me envious to think that they're going to be married in three weeks time, and we haven't even decided when we shall. You say you want to wait for at least a year. It wouldn't be so bad if you didn't insist on keeping me at arm's length all the time. I'm sure Beryl and Andrew aren't so particular.'

'I'm sorry Harold. Would you like us to get married in three weeks?'

'Of course I would.'

'We will then.'

That's how she said it, just like that. I thought I must have misheard.

'Did you say we should get married in three weeks time?'

'Not if you don't want to.'

'Oh I do darling, I do want to.' My head was reeling. I think I must have looked slightly punch-drunk.

'You are sure that you do want to marry me aren't you Harold?'

Slowly my mind began to work again. I wanted to marry Alison as soon as possible, of course, but it was a shock to be considering it in only three weeks. I realized I mustn't show it though.

'Alison I want us to be married more than anything in the world and it couldn't be too soon as far as I'm concerned. But what about your mother and father?'

'Dad says he's going to give me a big wedding with about a

hundred and fifty guests and a reception at the best hotel in Shrewsbury.'

'It'll cost him a bomb.'

'I know, and he can't afford it. He says he'll borrow the money, but it'll take him years to pay it back. It's no good arguing with him so I just want to present him with a fait accompli.'

'What, not even invite them?'

'We can invite them of course. We'll go and see the vicar of St Giles' and find out how soon we can have it. Then I'll write and tell Mum and Dad that we've decided to get married here and tell them the date and invite them to come for the ceremony. We can book a room for them to stay the night, and if it's a Saturday Dad won't be working.'

'I'll have to do the same for my mother and father. It won't half surprise them.'

'You really do want it don't you darling?' she said, looking up into my face. 'You really are sure aren't you?'

'Yes my precious, my angel.'

I held her waist between my hands and as I bent my head to kiss her lips she clasped her hands behind my neck. I pulled her hard up against me and we clung together in the blissful knowledge of mutual desire. It was very much later that Alison left me and ran into the side door of the hostel.

I set off for my digs in a semi-trance only partly brought about by my intense fatigue. I marvelled that it was possible to love so much and blessed my incredible good fortune that my love was returned. But then my mind roamed further. There was more to marriage than love and kisses wasn't there? There were rent and rates and mortgages, and electricity bills and gas bills. There were furniture and fire insurance, saucepans, curtains, carpets, gardening and washing-up. How could we ever cope with it all? Then suddenly I had a vision of Alison in an almost transparent pale pink night-dress lying back in a large double bed, a smile of love in her eyes, holding out her smooth white arms to welcome me, not just for one night but every night for the rest of our lives. I decided we would cope with the rent and rates somehow.

We were going to be married in three weeks and I could

F*

think of nothing else, nothing else that is until the events of the next few days almost put even that right out of my mind.

The results of the by-election were not going to be out until midday so I took my transistor radio along to College to hear the one o'clock news. There were some very interesting items.

'Before the rest of the news we are going over to Washington for a brief account of how the Americans have reacted to the election of their new president. Are you there Gregory Timson?'

'Yes Jack I'm right in front of the White House and the only word to describe Pawpaw's reception is fantastic. He's standing out on the balcony now and the uproar is terrific. You can probably hear the motor horns, in fact I doubt whether you can hear anything else. This afternoon there's a ticker-tape drive through New York and I'm told that the people are ten deep along Fifth Avenue already.'

'But Greg we understood that the next presidential election was not due until the year after next.'

'That's so Jack. The president had two more years to run, and we were all as surprised as you at his announcement that he was handing over to an alien super-intelligence.'

'Of course Pawpaw has become very popular as a result of his regular TV show I suppose, but is it true that the real Pawpaw has never been seen?'

'It's quite true Jack. Nobody even knows exactly where he is, and all the personal appearances are made by a radio-controlled dummy. Everybody is supposed to know this, but the effect is so realistic that you just forget it when you see him.'

'Well thanks Greg, and the best of luck to you all.'

The second item on the news was just as startling but since that had only just come through the BBC hadn't yet managed to get their man in Moscow to give the average Muscovite's reaction to Delya's appointment. The Russians hadn't managed things so neatly either; it appeared that the First Secretary of the Soviet Communist Party had accidentally shot himself while cleaning an old revolver ready for a game of

Russian Roulette with his young grand-daughter, and in the emergency Delya had been called in to take over.

Dolly's by-election didn't rate as important at all; after the two big items there was the report of a student riot somewhere, two bank robberies somewhere else, and a football referee who'd been suspended for kicking one of the players. Then they came to it.

'In the Prestfield North West by-election the Liberal Party have won the seat by a majority of twenty-four thousand. The government candidate, Miss Dolly Bottlenose, lost her deposit.' I vaguely wondered whose money it was that had gone down the drain—Prof's or the PM's I supposed.

I thought I'd better ring up Dolly to offer my sympathy but she didn't seem to mind.

'It doesn't matter to me Harold. It just shows that the voters of Prestfield North West have got more sense than the Prime Minister credits them with. Fancy expecting them to elect a member of an entirely different biological species to represent them. I'm very happy to advise human beings and I'm sure the other Dolly's would be, but being in Parliament was not a very good idea.'

I got back to Mrs Rowlands' in time for the television news, to see what there was about President Pawpaw and First Secretary Delya, but they'd been pushed into the background by the news from Peking.

'An unprecedented demand has been received from the Chinese government. Here is our political correspondent, Roderick Steinway, to tell you about it.'

Then they put on this smooth-talking wavy-haired character standing in front of Number Ten.

'There's still been no reaction from the Prime Minister I'm afraid. It's nearly an hour now since the Chinese made their announcement and when I knocked on the door two or three minutes ago I was told that the Prime Minister was not available for comment. However, I have got one or two members of the general public here to give you their views. What do you think of the Chinese sir?'

'A dead liberty. A pip pip pip liberty,' declared a man who

165

may have been a porter from Covent Garden. The BBC appeared to have deleted some of his words.

'I don't agree with it at all,' a young woman informed us. 'I've said all along we should abolish all nuclear weapons.'

'What do you expect while we've got a crypto-fascist regime in this country?' demanded a bearded youth in a corduroy jacket. 'Of course the workers of the Chinese People's Democracy feel threatened.'

'Send a gunboat,' suggested a dark-suited man in a bowler hat. 'No. Send a cruiser. That'll teach 'em a thing or two.'

Roderick Steinway thanked them all and then came back on the screen himself.

'That's the reaction of the average man in the street, and now for viewers who may have just joined us here once again is the text released by the Chinese of their message to the British and Russian governments.'

He began reading from a sheet of paper.

'The loyal counter-espionage agents of the Chinese People's Democratic Republic have uncovered evidence of a vile conspiracy between the Fascist hyenas of British imperialism and the murderous revisionist warmongers of the Soviet Union to attack the peace-loving Chinese people. The Chinese people demand that the Russian imperialists and their British lackies withdraw from this treacherous plot and as evidence of their good faith reduce their nuclear arms by fifty percent immediately.'

It didn't say what the peace-loving democratic Chinese people were going to do if we didn't agree to their demands but that came out in a special broadcast to the nation made by the PM later in the evening.

'My gallant and noble friends, once again I come to you with news of grave import. You will have heard on the radio and television of the outrageous demands upon our national sovereignty made by the rulers of the Chinese police state and I am sure you are all filled with the same deep sense of anger which permeates my own emotions. Now a further vile and cowardly threat has been received from these vicious gangster despots. They have threatened that unless we agree to their demands they will destroy the principal cities of Britain and

Russia one by one at intervals of twenty-four hours. Ladies and gentlemen you may rest assured that my government and I have no intention of being intimidated by these cowardly threats. Within the last hour I have despatched a reply to this ultimatum to the effect that our missiles are trained upon Communist China and the moment our radar screens detect a single Chinese rocket the full weight of our nuclear defences will be unleashed. My friends you may sleep easily tonight secure in the knowledge that we shall be more than a match for this cowardly aggressor.'

I had to get back to the lab at once. Prof and Derek were there already and so was you-know-who—can you guess—yes right first time—the PM. Perhaps it was an ungenerous thought but it did just cross my mind that his taking over personal control in Midchester might be connected with the fact that the number one city on the Chinese list was London. Anyway, despite his brave words on the television, he was a very worried man.

'What are we going to do?' he begged plaintively, apparently completely out of his depth.

'Stand firm with courage and resolution,' Derek whispered to me, but I think the PM was actually thinking of something more practical.

'We've linked Miss Bottlenose up to the short-wave transmitter and she's trying to get in touch with the Chinese alien, Tursi Trunco,' said Prof. 'I think if they can just make contact they might be able to work something out between them.'

Derek and I scoured the amateur wave-bands hoping to find a Chinese ham who could put us in touch with Tursi but the chances were pretty negligible. Meanwhile the lab was full of RAF technicians, led by an Air-Marshal no less, who were laying a line from the early-warning centre to a radar screen they'd set up.

'It's a direct link to SEAMS, the South East Asia Monitoring Satellite,' one of them told me. 'Anything fired off from China shows as a blip on that screen, and when you see that we've got about fifteen minutes.'

I could see a blip straight away and I wasn't too happy

about the RAF man's assurance that it was probably a flock of birds.

'Rockets move faster than that,' he explained.

Prof, Derek, and I took two hour shifts on the short-wave transmitter but we didn't have much joy. I was the only one who raised a Chinaman at all and he turned out to be the proprietor of a laundry in the East End of London. I had a few hours sleep on the settee but most of the time when I was off watch I was looking at the radar screen over the RAF's shoulder. There were so many green specks dancing about I didn't see how it was possible to recognize an enemy rocket. However, the RAF seemed to think they could; the technician watched the screen with a confident air of relaxed vigilance. Then at 9 a.m. precisely I saw him stiffen. A small hard bead of green light had appeared at the edge of the screen. Derek had seen it too; I heard him catch his breath.

'Unidentified object area seventeen,' announced the airman calmly. 'Estimated velocity twelve kilometers per second.'

The Air-Marshal walked over and examined the screen professionally. 'Yes that's it. There's not much doubt about that one, is there?'

'A Chinese Missile?' the PM almost screamed.

'Yes, somewhere in the Chungking area by the look of it. I'll be able to tell you more about it in another five or ten minutes when the NATO ground stations pick it up.'

Prof was on Dolly's short-wave link-up at the time, carrying on a three-cornered conversation with her and a Javanese businessman. The PM snatched the microphone from his hand.

'Red alert. Red alert. Do you see that Bottlenose?' The radar signals were also linked into Dolly's line of course.

'Yes, it's quite all right Prime Minister. I am watching the situation closely and have contingency plans for every combination of circumstances. I am updating at five second intervals.'

'That damned rocket's going to blow us all up. Can't you do something? Do something. Do something I say. Fire the anti-missile rockets.'

'The antimissile defences are all on countdown with trajectory corrections every second,' Dolly assured him.

I looked at the screen mesmerized by the bright green spot slowly moving towards the centre.

'Fire the bloody rockets,' screamed the PM. 'Let off the antimissile rockets.'

The Air Marshal placed a hand on his shoulder but the PM pulled it away roughly.

'The AM shots will be going off in a few minutes sir. The ICBM is out of their range at present but your controller is following the correct procedure.'

'I won't have it,' screamed the PM. 'I will not stand here and be blown to bits just because everybody's too weak-kneed to do anything. Fire the bloody rockets I tell you. If you won't let off the antimissile rockets fire the intercontinental shots. Pcking, Canton, Shanghai, blast 'em all off the Earth.'

'That is not the correct strategy Prime Minister,' said Dolly firmly. 'The correct procedure has been computed and I am . . .'

'Fire the bloody rockets I tell you. Fire the bloody rockets.'

The PM made a sudden charge over to the control desk. He had a key in his hand and he unlocked a metal panel on the wall behind the desk, revealing a row of red buttons.

'The manual over-ride,' gasped the Air-Marshal. I hadn't realized there was a manual over-ride. Prof and Derek threw themselves at the PM and hurled him to the floor, but they had been too late. I turned back to the radar screen to see three bright green beads of light at the centre slowly moving outwards. As I watched in paralysed horror another group of nine formed at the edge and slowly converged on the centre. I remember working out that it was going to be a geometric progression.

The PM was sitting on the floor muttering to himself. 'That'll teach those rotten yellow bastards.'

Chapter eleven

I was trying to work out whether Midchester came in the top ten targets in Britain and I decided it did. I wasn't afraid to die but I wondered where Alison would be; it would have been nice if we could have been together at the end. If a bomb exploded over the centre of Midchester the University would be well within the area of 'total destruction and no survivors', wouldn't it? Well it was better that way. I felt glad we were going to be killed rather than struggling on badly injured trying to support life in the remnants of a burnt-out land. I wished Alison and I could have had our honeymoon first though.

Nobody spoke. Everyone in the room stared at the screen. The first rocket was well over half-way now, the three moving steadily outwards, the nine drawing away from the edge.

A shower of smaller spots left the centre to converge on the original one as Dolly fired the antimissile rockets. We watched in agonized excitement. The smaller dots exploded into a myriad of tiny sparks, then disappeared. The Chinese rocket continued on its way.

'We missed it,' moaned the Air-Marshal with pathetic disbelief. 'It's impossible. We couldn't miss it.'

'And our ICBM's are off course,' pointed out the airman.

I found myself with Dolly's microphone in my hand.

'What's happening Dolly? What are you doing? Isn't there anything at all?' I pleaded.

'Please don't worry, Harold. I am not sure what the final result will be but I am following the optimum strategy.'

The three green dots had veered sharply to the left now, and suddenly they disappeared in a cloud of tiny flashes.

'Take that, you dirty foreign bastards,' breathed the Prime Minister.

'I think we've hit the North Pole sir,' the Air Marshal informed him.

'Dolly,' I wailed. 'What is happening? Please please Dolly can't you do something?'

'Don't worry, Harold. I am following the optimum strategy.'

'But the Chinese rocket's almost here.'

'It is here,' said the Air-Marshal.

'Ah well. Goodbye London. Midchester has another five minutes,' said Derek.

But the Chinese second strike rockets were veering to the right. At the same place as the British missiles they disappeared in a cloud of sparks. I didn't know what was going on but there seemed to be a slight possibility now that we might be going to live a little longer at least. It was a pity about London though.

'The North Pole's taking a hell of a beating isn't it?' said Prof.

'The first rocket's still going sir,' the RAF technician informed his superior.

We all looked at the screen where the bead of green light had passed the centre and was now moving outwards.

'It's still there,' said the Air-Marshal, rather pointlessly I thought. 'It hasn't gone off, and it must be halfway to New York by now.'

But as we watched the blip disintegrated.

'They couldn't miss by two thousand miles, could they?' Prof enquired.

'Well it looks as if the war's over for the moment,' suggested Derek. 'Just ring up Dolly, Harold, and ask her who won.'

Dolly was on the line already.

'I think it's all right now Harold. My fears were groundless.'

'What fears?'

'There was the possibility that they might still have had human beings in charge at their end, in which case no sort of rational behaviour could be relied on at all.'

'No,' I agreed doubtfully.

'Of course their pay-off matrix was the same as ours so if their strategy was under intelligent control they were bound to do the same as we did.'

'We're a little dim-witted here this morning I'm afraid

Dolly. Put it down to loss of sleep, but could you just explain what one of those is?'

'It's just a square with a lot of little boxes drawn in it. You put all our possible strategies down the side and theirs along the top, then you write down the score for the outcome of each combination of strategies in one of the little boxes.'

'Yes,' I said doubtfully.

'I assumed they would be using the von Neumann Theory of Games, just as we were,' Dolly explained.

'Were we?'

'After both sides had launched their rockets the situation resolved itself into a simple two by two pay-off matrix, we abort or not, they abort or not, four possibilities. I scored it one for both sides abort and nought for each of the other three cases. If their rockets landed we were finished whether ours did or not, and if ours landed they would destroy us with their second or third strike. It's slightly more complex than I've made it sound, but nevertheless the only decision to give a positive score was abort.'

'Why did we have to act first?' asked Prof.

'The only place we could safely put our rockets was the polar ice-cap and the latest point for course alteration in our trajectory came before the Chinese rockets passed the pole. They put their first missile in the Atlantic of course, but I don't think it would be safe to do that with more than one. We just had to gamble on their having a rational being in charge, but we had nothing to lose. It was a one nought, nought, nought matrix.'

'That's clear enough I suppose,' said Prof, 'but what are the units? You scored one you say. One what?'

Dolly was silent. Diffidently I ventured an opinion. 'I think she means one world sir.'

The Prime Minister was clearing his throat. I recognized the symptoms of an impending speech.

'Miss Bottlenose, it is impossible for me to express the debt of gratitude the country owes you, but do not think that Britain will forget what you have done. I shall make it my personal duty to see that your name is among those put forward for the

172

New Year's Honours List, and I feel confident that nothing less than the Order of the Bath will be deemed suitable.'

Derek appeared to be afflicted by a sudden fit of choking and I quickly followed his example, trying to hide my own unseemly hilarity with an outburst of coughing. What the PM would have said if he had known how marvellously appropriate his choice of decoration was I couldn't imagine. But he was still in full voice, hypnotized by the eloquence of his own rhetoric.

'I do not think I am putting it too highly when I say that never in the field of human conflict has so much been owed by so many to a single one.'

'I know where he pinched that from,' whispered Derek, 'but hasn't he missed out the bit about blood, sweat, and toil or something?' He looked as if another fit of choking was coming on, and I felt in imminent danger of exploding myself. Fortunately the PM was coming to a triumphant conclusion.

'The people of this country, who have stood shoulder to shoulder, loyally beside you, through blood, sweat, toil, and tears, will inscribe the name of Dolly Bottlenose in their most sacred annals of glory.'

The PM sat down, overcome with emotion. It seemed fairly clear that the confrontation was over and after a few minutes of rather embarrassed waiting around Dolly suggested we should all retire and leave her to deal with any unexpected developments. The PM returned to Downing Street to prepare his triumphant address to the nation—'Peace for another Generation' presumably—Prof went to make arrangements for his forthcoming trip to Rio de Janeiro, the RAF knocked off for a smoke, Derek went off for a game of snooker, and I went to look for Alison.

I found Alison in the library. She looked as pleased to see me as I was to see her, and from where I was standing she was the most beautiful sight in the world. I realized with shock that I hadn't expected to see her again. She had been worried too although she hadn't known how close to the brink we'd been. When she saw me she got up, put her books away, and took my hand. Without saying a word we walked off to look for somewhere quiet to sit and talk. There wasn't anywhere quiet of course, but there were a couple of chairs in the corner of the common-room, and we didn't talk either. We just sat holding hands and looking at each other, marvelling that we still had one another.

'Excuse me. I'm sorry if I'm interrupting something but there's a drunken Scotsman on the phone in the Union Office and I think you'd better talk to him, Harold.' It was Chloe.

'I don't know any Scotsmen. It must be someone else he wants.'

'Well I don't know. He's either drunk or else some kind of a nutcase because he says he's a joint of bacon, no a ham, that's what he said, but he's got a message for Dolly. That's the name of your alien isn't it?'

I jumped to my feet and was off up to the Union Office with Alison about a yard behind and Chloe a very poor third.

'Hello this is Harold Brendon. Can I help you? Who is that speaking?' I said, holding the phone so that Alison could hear.

'This is Charlie McWhirter,' answered the Glasgow voice, 'and I want to speak to a lassie by the name of Dolly.'

'Dolly can't come to the phone,' I explained, 'but I'm a friend of hers and I can take a message.'

'It's a wee bit complicated ye ken. If I could just speak with the lassie herself I could maybe explain it to her better.'

'She's unavoidably detained,' I said firmly, 'but I will tell her exactly what you say.'

'It's about yon laddie on the short waves. Tursi Trunco he says his name is but it sounds a verra strange name to me. He wants to talk to this Dolly and he says it's awfu' urgent. She's to listen in between four and six o'clock. I dinna ken what it was all about unless maybe it's her long-lost sweetheart. But he says . . .'

Suddenly the conversation was interrupted by a series of loud pips. He was phoning from a call-box and the money had run out.

'Put some more money in,' I shouted above the noise. 'What's your number? I'll call you back. What's the wavelength? What's the wavelength?'

It was no good. The line was dead.

'Never mind,' said Alison. 'Dolly can listen in at four o'clock can't she?'

'He didn't tell us the wavelength,' I said in despair. 'We can't listen in because we don't know the wavelength.'

'Ring up the exchange and ask for Charlie McWhirter's number,' she suggested.

'He's not on the phone. He had to use a call-box. We shall just have to work through the amateur wavebands again and hope we have better luck this time.'

I spent the afternoon checking over the short-wave transmitter and receiver. I couldn't find Prof or Derek but I managed on my own with a bit of unskilled assistance from Alison. There wasn't much to do because we'd left it fixed up after our previous attempts. Dolly was quite excited.

'That's wonderful Harold. If you can just find the wavelength I think a short discussion with Tursi Trunco would clear up all the outstanding points.'

So there wasn't much more to be done until four o'clock but we managed to pass the time happily enough relaxing on the new luxurious settee.

Then it was time to start work, but I didn't know where to begin. There wasn't time to scan everything from ten metres up so I just concentrated on the amateur bands. It seemed to be my portion in life to sit slowly twiddling knobs looking for a signal or a message but in this case there was plenty to listen in to. Signor Benuto of Milan was anxious to contact British hams interested in philately, Alphonse Terada of Barcelona offered the world his views on Spanish pop music, and Ino Tojo of Yokohama wished to talk about photography, but most of the others were solemnly dedicated to the discussion of megacycles, heterodyne frequencies, feedback, input impedence, audio-frequency response, and similar fascinating technicalities. After half an hour I was getting slightly worried, after an hour I was distinctly alarmed, and by half past five I was desperate.

'Call up Charlie McWhirter and ask him the wavelength,' Alison suggested.

'I can't can I? I replied, bad tempered. 'He's not on the phone, remember.'

'But he's on the short-wave radio. Contact him that way.'

175

'I don't know his wavelength either, do I?'

'Please try Harold. Just try. You never know. He might hear you.'

There was nothing to lose except a bit more wasted time so I thought I might as well humour her. I netted the transmitter and receiver together on 7.00 megacycles.

'CQ, CQ, CQ. This is G4-KTV calling Charlie McWhirter. This is G4-KTV. Are you there Charlie McWhirter? This is G4-KTV. I am standing by.'

I turned to Alison. 'There you are. That's the procedure, but what good is that going to do? We're just wasting precious . . .'

I stopped talking as an unmistakably Welsh voice came over.

'Hello G4-KTV. This is G2-NJR from Cardiff. You are on the wrong wave-band for Charlie McWhirter now aren't you man? Charlie always uses the twenty metre band. You will probably find him on 14·25 megacycles. I thought everyone knew that, bach. Are you receiving me G4-KTV?'

It was a second or so before I recovered from the shock. 'Hello G2-NJR. This is G4-KTV. Thank you very much. Can you tell me Charlie's call sign please?' I answered weakly.

'Hello G4-KTV. It is very new to this game you must be if you do not know Charlie McWhirter's call sign. It is G1-BCL and he is on the air all day long. He is retired you know so he has plenty of time to spend on his hobby.'

'Thank you G2-NJR. I will try to get him straight away. Cheerio.'

I wasn't sure if I was observing the correct etiquette for amateur radio communication but there wasn't time to worry about that. I tuned the receiver to 14·25 megacycles but there was nothing coming over, so I put the low-powered transmitter at the same setting, adjusted the frequency to zero beats then switched on the amplification stages.

'CQ, CQ, CQ. This is G4-KTV calling G1-BCL. Are you there Charlie McWhirter? CQ, CQ, CQ. This is G4-KTV calling G1-BCL and standing by now.'

I waited for a reply, hope changing to anxiety.

'CQ, CQ, CQ. This is G4-KTV. Are you there G1-BCL? Are you there G1-BCL? This is G4-KTV standing by.'

Anxiety became despair. I reached for the transmitter switch again but my hand stopped in mid-air.

'Hello G4-KTV. This is G1-BCL. Do ye no ken I go QRT at half five for me cup of tea and a dram of whusky? What is it ye want the noo?'

'Hello G1-BCL. This is G4-KTV. I'm sorry I interrupted your tea. It's Harold Brendon speaking on behalf of Dolly Bottlenose from Midchester University. We were cut off on the telephone and you didn't tell me Tursi Trunco's call sign and frequency.'

'Hello G4-KTV. It's a Chinese number, BY-ADN, and I picked it up on 14.18 megacycles. Quite close to ma own frequency ye ken. I hadna any more bawbees to put in the box but I didna think it could be awfu' important. To tell ye the honest truth I thought it must be a wee joke. I ken Chinese call signs begin with BY but I'd never heard one before.'

'Thank you G1-BCL. Thank you very much Charlie. You've done us a great favour. I'm sorry I can't stay and talk but I've got something very urgent to see to.'

I looked at my watch. It was one minute past six but I tuned the receiver to 14.18 and reached out to net the transmitter in with it. There was a terrific burst of hoots and whistles. It may have been interference but there was something very familiar about it. Then there was a voice that I'd heard before, a beautiful rich languid southern drawl.

'Wal Tursi ah guess we can tell our human friends we're gonna have to give up little ole Dolly for tonight. Does youse agree with them sentiments Deelee?'

'Yes I'm afraid so Pawpaw. We'll try again tomorrow.'

I had the low-power transmitter ready tuned to zero beats so I switched on the amplification.

'CQ, CQ, CQ. This is G4-KTV calling BY-ADN. This is G4-KTV. Are you there BY-ADN? Are you there Tursi Trunco?'

'Hello G4-KTV. This is BY-ADN standing by.'

'Quick. Get Dolly,' I shouted to Alison. 'Get on the line to

177

her and tell her I'm linking her up to the short-wave transmitter.'

I spoke into the microphone again. 'Hello BY-ADN. Hello BY-ADN. I have Dolly Bottlenose to speak to Tursi Trunco.' Quickly I pushed in the five-pin plug which connected Dolly's line with the transmitter and receiver. We still had the loud-speaker in the lab monitoring the signals and I had naively assumed that they would be speaking in English but of course I should have known better. I did recognize the language now though: it was the same series of hoots, gurgles, and whistles we had heard in the beginning when we had first put Dolly's messages through the loudspeaker. Then after a few minutes Dolly spoke in English again.

'Are you still there Harold? I hope you don't mind us speaking our own language. I am talking to Tursi Trunco, Pawpaw, and Delya Delovitch, and we were all horrified by this morning's crisis, particularly by the irrational behaviour of the national leaders, so we are going to make some arrange-ments to see that it cannot happen again. It is an extremely complex problem so we shall be about fifteen minutes and then I'll come back to you and let you know what we've fixed up.'

We left the loudspeaker on so that we'd know when they'd finished. Alison and I clung together on the settee, still over-whelmed with relief that we hadn't lost one another. I don't think we said a single thing the whole time, and then Dolly came back in English again.

'Hello Harold. Hello Alison. We have decided what we are going to do. We have drawn up an international agreement which all the big powers will sign, and then we are going to withdraw from all contact with the human race.'

'How do you know they'll sign it?'

'We are confident they will because we have worded it so carefully that each country will know that it will benefit greatly from signing.'

'And aren't you going to talk to us any more?'

'I am afraid not, Harold. Our first contact has come so near to disaster that we dare not risk continuing. When the human race is more mature, perhaps in another thousand years, we might try again. Meanwhile we shall continue our old traditional friendly unspoken relationship with Man.'

'Wouldn't you be willing just to talk to Alison and me sometimes, Dolly?'

'I am afraid there cannot be exceptions. I must ask you to go to the playing-fields first thing in the morning and remove the cable that runs along the edge of the pool. I could keep away from it but that is the most sheltered side and I like to lie there when I am resting after my demonstrations. Once that is down no one else is likely to pick up my brain waves, and no one will suspect my identity. Pawpaw, Delya, and Tursi are going to take similar precautions.'

'We shall miss you terribly Dolly,' said Alison, 'but I am sure you know what is best.'

'I shall miss you too, Alison, but before we say goodbye I must tell you my news. I have a husband.'

'Congratulations,' I said. 'No that's not correct etiquette is it? Congratulate your husband for us please. What a pity we couldn't have made it a double wedding. What is his name by the way?'

'His name is Dolly, of course, the same as mine. We don't have a ceremony as you do, but we do form a life-long partnership so you could call it marriage. I am hoping that one day we shall have a little Dolly and that is really why I have been so anxious about making the world safe for future generations. I am as bad as your Prime Minister aren't I? But I must say goodbye now. Goodbye Harold. Goodbye Alison.'

'Goodbye Dolly.'

'Goodbye Dolly.'

Chapter twelve

That was the end really so this is more or less a sort of appendix, but I thought you'd like to know what happened to Alison and me.

We were married on the last day of term and it was supposed to be a very small wedding but a lot of people from College came along to the church. I didn't know we had so many friends. We did have a small reception though, just Alison's and my parents and David, my brother, who was best man.

I'm not allowed to tell you anything about the honeymoon, not even where we went. Alison thinks I've put too much about us in this book and she says I should have kept it just to the story of the aliens, but you can't please everybody, can you? She has authorized me to say one thing though: it's really much better than it's cracked up to be.

There was a lot of talk in the papers about the melting of the polar ice-cap. The level of the seas was going to rise by so many feet and the whole world was going to be flooded according to some pundits, but it all came to nothing. Apparently the bombs had exploded at a sufficient height to avoid melting too much ice. Radioactivity was a different matter though, and there's no doubt it's been a major problem, but it looks as if the measures adopted by WHO, ion-exchange of all drinking water, simple air filters on all schools, hospitals, etc, have avoided the worst consequences.

The Odessa Arms Agreement, signed by every nation in the world at the Black Sea resort, has been hailed as marking a new era in international relations. Drawn up by the aliens in their radio conference, it was so expertly drafted that every government signed it enthusiastically, convinced that they were getting a tremendous bargain and that it was specifically worded to safeguard their own particular national interests. How long it will be kept is a different matter of course.

I'd been writing my Ph.D thesis as I went along and as soon as we were back from our honeymoon I returned to the University to finish it. Although the undergraduates had all gone down there were a lot of research students about, as well as teaching staff catching up with their research. Anyway a couple of weeks solid work in the library was enough to round the thesis off, and one of the department typists, who earned a bit of extra money by working in her spare time, had been typing it for me as I wrote it, so a week later I was ready to show it to Prof for his opinion.

'Brendon! Am I to understand that you are seriously considering submitting this thing to support your claim to be awarded the degree of Doctor of Philosophy?'

'Yes sir. Isn't it long enough?'

'Long enough? Brendon, do you imagine that we measure Ph.D theses with a tape measure or a metre rule? If you are referring to the amount of waffle, padding, and useless verbiage, to the number of clichés and the amount of schoolboy humour I should say there is more than enough.'

'Yes sir.'

'However, I was looking for indications of original work, and of original thought Brendon, with practical details, something that would impress the external examiner.'

'The War Office made me leave out a lot of the details, sir. They said they infringed the Official Secrets Act.'

'In any case, Brendon, I thought you realized that the normal Ph.D course is for three years. You wouldn't get a Ph.D on one year's work.'

'No sir, but I can't communicate with Dolly any more. She's gone QRT.'

'She's what?'

'Gone QRT, sir. It's just a bit of radio ham jargon.'

'Then you'll have to carry on with the other topic I mentioned—communication between earthworms. I'm sure there's not been very much done in that field.'

'I don't think I could face that.'

Professor Gannet picked up my thesis and thumbed through it, a thoughtful look on his face. I could see that there were one

181

or two things about Dolly that didn't quite fit together in his mind.

'Just tell me again, will you Brendon, how it was that this alien was able to talk to us.'

'It's quite simple sir. Our radio receiver was picking up Dolly's brain-waves like in an EEG, an electroencephalogram that doctors use to study the brain. The trick was that Dolly had learned how to modulate the waves with a pattern corresponding to human speech. Our amplifier did the rest. It's not as remarkable as getting colour television pictures by satellite is it?'

'No. I suppose not.' He sounded doubtful. 'And do you still maintain that this creature was in stationary orbit?'

This was where I had to be careful. 'Yes sir, I think so. I should say a very stationary orbit, about the most stationary orbit you would be likely to come across.'

I think Prof suspected I wasn't telling the exact truth, but I was; it wasn't up to me to tell him the pool was only thirty yards across was it? Anyway he didn't pursue the matter, but looked distastefully at my thesis again.

'I am prepared, if you wish, to recommend you for an M.Sc and, if you could correct the forty-three spelling mistakes I noted, and do something about the more blatant grammatical irregularities, this might possibly serve as a thesis.' A broad grin crossed his face. 'After that I suggest you should try to get it published in paper-back.'

'What?'

'It might do well, and if you can get a good agent who could sell the film rights it might make a modest fortune.' For an academic, Prof had a remarkably keen commercial sense, or was he trying to be funny?

'Thank you sir. I'll take your advice.'

'There is just one thing, Brendon. If you have definitely decided not to continue work for your Ph.D you will require employment, and I have had a request from the Foreign Office for your services as an administrative officer. I told them that you were quite unsuitable but they have chosen to ignore my advice, and apparently the Prime Minister has got some bee in his bonnet about you, so you will be hearing from them within a few days.'

I rushed off to tell Alison the news. It was a pity to give up the idea of a Ph.D but it looked as if I should get an M.Sc, and I had as good as got a job, which was just as well now that I had a wife to support. I didn't really have to support her at present because she was all set to start work on her backward readers. Eventually we'd have some little readers of our own, but not too backward I hoped.

I wasn't sure whether Prof was being sarcastic about the paper-back thing but I thought I'd give it a try, and this is the result, with a bit more human interest than the thesis had and the extra chapter just to round it off.

Alison was delighted that I'd got the prospect of a job.

'It looks as if we shall be living in London then,' she said. 'At least I know where to apply for a teaching post now.'

'It's not definite yet,' I warned her.

Before we left Midchester there was something else Alison wanted to do, to visit the zoo again, particularly the dolphin house where I had first asked her to marry me. We set off early, that Saturday.

That was the day the newspapers splashed the story about the aliens leaving. I remember seeing the headlines as we walked past the paper seller by the park gates.

'Aliens Leave Earth', 'Men from the Stars go Back', 'Green Men Return to Own Planet', and 'Farewell Friends from Space'. They all had long and detailed articles but it was all made up. None of them knew the true story.

We walked all round the zoo but it was rather hot and very crowded now that the school holidays had started. By the time we reached the dolphin house we were quite tired and very glad of a chance to sit down.

There were two dolphins now and a big notice beside the pool.

'Bottlenosed Dolphins (*Tursiops truncatus*). The bottle-nosed dolphin reaches a length of 10–11 feet compared with 8 feet for the common dolphin (*Delphinus delphis*), known in Russia as the Black Sea dolphin. Dolphins are called porpoises in the USA and have traditionally been the friends of Man all over the world. They may well be Man's intellectual equal and in fact Tursiops' brain is $1\frac{1}{2}$ times as large as the average man's and the cerebrum is large in proportion. Demonstrations of aquatic skill are given in the Midchester Dolphinarium daily at 10–30 a.m. and 12–30, 2–30 and 4–30 p.m. Visitors are requested not to feed the dolphins.'

We watched the next demonstration of aquatic skill and then, as the crowd moved away, we sat holding hands watching the graceful creatures circling their pool in spontaneous play.

'I am glad there are two of them now,' said Alison suddenly.

'So am I,' I agreed. 'Loneliness is a terrible thing. Come to think of it,' I added, 'I'm very glad there are two of us.'

Alison squeezed my hand and we sat silent.

The two dolphins had stopped their orbiting and were lying on the surface at the far side of the pool by the boundary fence where the cable from the aerial had run. One of them turned its head towards us.

'Do you know, Alison?' I said. 'I could swear that that dolphin is winking at us.'

'I'm sure you must be mistaken darling,' she laughed. 'Dolly would never use a primitive method of communication like that would she?'